KISSES SWEETER THAN WINE

A RIVER WINERY NOVEL

JEN TALTY

KISSES SWEETER THAN WINE

A Candlewood Falls Novel
The River Winery Series

by
USA Today Bestselling Author
JEN TALTY

This is a work of fiction. Names, characters, places, and incidents are the product of the author's imagination or are used fictitiously. Any resemblance to actual persons, living or dead, or actual events or locales is entirely coincidental.

Kisses Sweeter than Wine

Copyright © 2022 by Jen Talty

Printed in the USA

"*Deadly Secrets* is the best of romance and suspense in one hot read!" *NYT Bestselling Author Jennifer Probst*

"A charming setting and a steamy couple heat up the pages in a suspenseful story I couldn't put down!" *NY Times and USA today Bestselling Author Donna Grant*

"Jen Talty's books will grab your attention and pull you into a world of relatable characters, strong personalities, humor, and believable storylines. You'll laugh, you'll cry, and you'll rush to get the next book she releases!" Natalie Ann USA Today Bestselling Author

"I positively loved *In Two Weeks,* and highly recommend it. The writing is wonderful, the story is fantastic, and the characters will keep you coming back for more. I can't wait to get my hands on future installments of the NYS Troopers series." *Long and Short Reviews*

"*In Two Weeks* hooks the reader from page one. This is a fast paced story where the development of the romance grabs you emotionally and the suspense keeps you sitting on the edge of your chair. Great characters, great writing, and a believable plot that can be a warning to all of us." *Desiree Holt, USA Today Bestseller*

"*Dark Water* delivers an engaging portrait of wounded hearts as the memorable characters take you on a healing journey of love. A mysterious death brings danger and intrigue into the drama, while sultry passions brew into a believable plot that melts the reader's heart. Jen Talty pens an entertaining romance that grips the heart as the colorful and dangerous story unfolds into a chilling ending." *Night Owl Reviews*

"This is not the typical love story, nor is it the typical mystery. The characters are well rounded and interesting." *You Gotta Read Reviews*

"*Murder in Paradise Bay* is a fast-paced romantic thriller with plenty of twists and turns to keep you guessing until the end. You won't want to miss this one..." *USA Today bestselling author Janice Maynard*

HAVE WE GOT A STORY FOR YOU!

Dear Readers:

Welcome to Candlewood Falls!

Each Candlewood Falls story stands alone. However, the end of one story doesn't mean the end of your favorite characters. They can show up in any Candlewood Falls book at any time.

Candlewood Falls is a unique world of connected stories by different authors whose characters, business, and events appear in each others' stories.

Think of Candlewood Falls as a literary soap opera.

Be sure to check out the the other authors and discover which other books include your favorite characters.

Happy reading!

Stacey Wilk & K.M Fawcett & Jen Talty

I'm super excited about the rest of the River Family and their stories. Check these out by moi - Jen Talty *USA Today* Bestselling Author

There was one problem that stood in his way...and he was falling in love with her. RIVERS EDGE

Some truths weren't meant to be uncovered. THE BURIED SECRET

Where broken dreams collide, two hearts will come together and find the love they thought they lost. ITS IN HIS KISS

She was only supposed to help with his sone...only she showed him what family and love was truly about. LIPS OF AN ANGEL

For more Alpachino the Alpaca antics and to find out who went to prison for killing Sam's Father's read <u>TAKING ROOT</u> by Stacey Wilk.

And the second book in Stacey's series...What will Brad Wilde the man who has it all do when an orphan is dropped on his doorstep? RAISING WINTER by Stacey Wilk.

Also by Stacey Wilk in this series: Even the most unexpected circumstances may teach us how to forgive what cannot be changed. DEFINING CHANCES.

And While packing away her mothers life, Petra Wilde discovers a life of her own in BEGINNING OVER.

If you want to spend some time with Sam Wilde and his quest for an apple to make you happy and horny you'll want to read WILDE TEMPTATION by K.M. FAWCETT.

And the second book in K.M. Fawcett's series...Spend the holidays with Lacey Wilde, her dog Remi, and a sexy marine who claims Remi belongs to him in WILDE CHRISTMAS by K.M. Fawcett.

Also by K.M. Fawcett is WILD IN LOVE: Can a bad boy and a good girl overcome their fears to find true love?

And in WILDE TREASURES: While searching for a hidden fortune, can two lonely adventurers discover some treasurers are more precious than gold.

Thank you for visiting Candlewood Falls!

Be sure to leave a review to help readers like you find and enjoy our small town.

Join our exciting community of authors and readers at the Candlewood Falls Facebook Readers Group for cover reveals, sneak peaks, deleted scenes, and excerpts from upcoming releases. Plus games and fun!

ACKNOWLEDGMENTS

A big thank you to Stacey Wilk and K.M. Fawcett for inviting me into Candlewood Falls.

Twenty-One Years Ago...

Carter River glanced around the bus terminal three towns west of Candlewood Falls, still concerned they could be recognized. He handed a thick envelope to Heather. "This should be enough to get you started."

"I don't know how to repay you." Heather swiped the tears from her cheeks.

"Make a good life for you and Daisy. That's all I could ever ask for." Carter squeezed her biceps.

She glanced over her shoulder. "I'm scared. What if Richard finds out what we did?"

"He won't."

"But he's got friends in high places," Heather said.

"So do I and from this moment forward, you and Daisy are dead," Carter whispered. "Follow the directions I've given you. Once you meet your contact, you'll be given new identities. Everything will be okay."

Heather blew out a puff of air and squared her shoulders.

Carter had known her most of her life. She'd been a staple in the Candlewoods Falls community. How Richard had destroyed this woman's resolve had been more than a crime. It tortured Carter's soul that his son's girlfriend had experienced such horror at the hands of her father. If Carter had known sooner, maybe he could have done more.

But Heather and Daisy kept their shame hidden well.

"I wish Daisy could have said goodbye to Merlot. I know they're just kids, but she loves him so much. It will be so hard for her to get over him."

"He loves her too." Carter understood young love better than most. He'd been in love with Weezer his entire life. Their relationship didn't make sense to anyone but them and their family. He didn't care that people whispered behind their backs or poked fun at his wife. She was the glue that held his family together and would ensure that Merlot got through this trying time. "You better get on that bus."

"Thank you, Carter. From the bottom of my heart." Heather kissed his cheek. She turned, grabbed her bag and her daughter, and boarded the bus.

Carter had purchased a one-way ticket to get them to Chicago, where they'd meet someone he'd been in touch with in the underground to help them build their new life.

One far away from the abuse of Richard Berkin.

"You did the only thing you could." Weezer slipped her arm around his waist as the bus pulled out of the station. "They will be better off."

"But will our son?"

Merlot

Merlot River waited patiently for everyone to leave the gravesite before approaching the casket. He could feel his parents' gaze tear into his backside.

They'd said all the right things. They'd been loving and kind, like parents were supposed to be. They'd always supported his relationship with Daisy. They never belittled it or told him she wasn't good enough or the wrong girl for him.

Not like they had done with his other siblings and those they dated.

Daisy was different. Special. He knew without a shadow of a doubt that she'd been *the one.*

But that didn't change the fact that Daisy was dead and he wouldn't get to spend the rest of his life loving her. They wouldn't get to go to college together or return to Candlewood Falls and build a small house on the winery. They wouldn't work for the family business until it was time for them to have a family.

They had it all planned out and her father wouldn't stop them.

However, a tragedy changed everything.

The fire had been ruled an accident. The investigator stated it had been started in the kitchen—something about a faulty pilot on the stove.

Merlot struggled to believe it.

He placed the single tulip on the casket. Her favorite flower. Everyone thought she liked daisies because of her name, but she didn't. Tulips all the way. She used to joke her mom should have named her Tulip or Talulah. Staring at the casket, he conjured up their last time together. It had been the night before the fire. He'd told her he loved her and would always protect her.

He failed.

Miserably.

That very night, after he brought her home, her father went into a rage. He smacked her mother around and then put his hands on Daisy. His eyes burned, but he couldn't bring himself to cry. "I'm so sorry," he whispered.

"You should be," a deep voice rumbled.

He turned. The taste of bile filled his throat. His muscles twitched. Fear prickled the back of his neck as he stared at Daisy's father.

His friends joked about being afraid of his mother. How they never wanted to be on her bad side. Everyone in town had all heard the stories of Weezer chasing someone down Main Street in her housecoat, curlers, and combat boots while holding a loaded shotgun. His mom enjoyed her reputation and played into it. When Merlot was in grade school, he hated how the other children shied away from being his friend, but now that he was a senior in high school, he wore his family's strangeness like a badge of honor.

He squared his shoulders, doing his best to cover his fear.

"You've been nothing but trouble ever since you started coming around." Mr. Berkin inched closer. "My family is gone, and I blame you for this sham of a funeral. I'm surprised you didn't pretend to die with them."

There had never been any love lost between Merlot and Mr. Berkin. From the moment they'd met as small children, to when they started dating, Mr. Berkin did what he could to keep them apart. It had gotten so bad that they hid their relationship from her father. His family knew, and her mother did, but to keep the peace, they pretended they weren't a couple.

Until two months ago when Mr. Berkin caught them at the park. He'd been furious. The next day, Daisy didn't come to school. Later, Merlot found out it was because she had a black eye, thanks to her old man.

"I don't know what you're talking about." Merlot wiped the tears from his cheeks. Daisy wouldn't fake her death. That was insane and only happened in the movies. It didn't matter that they'd discussed the possibility, the idea that she'd do it without him made no sense.

"Right. Leave. You are not welcome here," Mr. Berkin said. "And if I ever catch you near this gravesite again, I'll beat your punk ass." He poked Merlot in the center of his chest.

"You touch my son again, and you will live to regret it." Merlot's father appeared at his side as if from nowhere. His dad tended to sneak up when he least expected it. He often hated that, but in this case, it was a welcome gesture. "That's not a threat. It's a promise."

Mr. Berkin raised his hands. "Just keep him away from my daughter's grave and we won't have a problem."

Merlot's father looped a protective arm around him and guided him toward the path. "I know you don't want to hear this, son, but I think it's best if you take heed and stay clear for a while."

"That man belongs in jail."

"I'm well aware of that fact," his father said. "But he didn't start that fire. That's something you need to accept, as hard as it is." His father squeezed his shoulder. "Grief isn't an easy thing and I wish I could tell you that it goes away. But you will get through this. If you can learn to see past all the anger and hurt, you will love again. You're seventeen years old. You have your entire life ahead of you. If the tables were turned, I know you'd want her to go on living and that's what you need to do."

Merlot wouldn't want Daisy pining for him for years and years. If he'd been the one who died, he'd absolutely want her to go out into the world and live a full life. It wouldn't be fair of him to expect anything else.

And it wouldn't be right.

Her kisses were sweeter than any wine his family could make, and living was the best way to pay homage to their love.

"I know," he managed. "But I feel like a horrible person for wishing it had been Mr. Berkin in that fire, and not Daisy and her mother."

"That doesn't make you a bad man, Merlot." His dad paused, taking him by the shoulders and locking gazes. "I've had many negative thoughts when it comes to Richard Berkin. He's not a nice person and I need you to keep your distance. You're going to be going away to college soon. There's a lot left to prepare for that."

School was the last thing on Merlot's mind, but he knew his parents meant well and wanted him to focus on the positive things in life, even though he couldn't think of one good thing.

His father paused, taking him by the shoulders. "I know the world feels like a grim place right now and will for a while." He placed his hand on the center of Merlot's chest. "No matter what happens to you in life, there will always be a part of Daisy that you carry with you. No one is telling you to let go of that. All I'm saying is that over time, this intense pain will be lifted and all the wonderful memories you have of her will be something you can look back on and cherish."

Merlot wanted to believe his father. However, it felt like his heart burned in the fire with Daisy.

PRESENT DAY

TALBOT

Talbot Grant unlocked the door to the rental her boss, Claudia, had secured. She stepped into the modest home and glanced around. "What the heck?" The place was filled with—dare she think it—junk. It looked like everything had been pulled from a dumpster.

She sneezed, thanks to the inch of dust piled on everything. It would take her hours to clean this place up to make it habitable.

It reminded her of the first month she and her mother had fled Candlewood Falls, a place she'd promised her mother she'd never, under any circumstance, ever set foot in again, much less come back and spend a month.

She ripped off her big hat, tossing it to the ugly

brown sofa in the middle of the family room. Pushing her oversized sunglasses, which were way too big for her face, to the top of her head, she rolled her suitcase around countless knickknacks and crap until she found the master bedroom.

If one could call it that.

Not that Talbot was used to the finer things. However, ever since her son, Corbin, had been born, she'd lived in a hotel, which came with some perks.

"Holy shit." She stood at the edge of the saggy bed. "The things I do for you, Claudia," she muttered. Of course, her boss had no idea Talbot was originally from Candlewood Falls. Or that her birth name had been something else.

That person died twenty-one years ago.

But being back in this small, sleepy town, the first seventeen years of her life came crashing down on her brain like a penny dropping from the top of the Empire State Building.

Living a lie had been the easy part. She'd been doing that her entire life. She'd covered for her father and his sins as a kid. However, falling in love with Merlot changed everything. He made her want to modify the direction of her life. She had no idea that meant she'd have to give him up.

Forever.

Her cell rang. She raced through the house, stumbling over an oddly placed piece of furniture. Whoever lived here before her had an odd sense of taste. "Hello?"

"Hey, Talbot. Are you in Candlewood Falls yet?" Claudia asked.

"Just arrived at the rental. By chance did the owner send you pictures? Because this place is where murders happen."

Claudia laughed. "You're always so dramatic. I'm sure it's not that bad."

"It looks like it hasn't been cleaned in months. Is there someone I can call? I can clean it myself, but considering you paid for a month's lease, the owner should have at least run a damn vacuum."

"I'll text you Andy Johnson's contact information. He's who I sent the check to and I believe he's the owner. I'm sure he'll take care of it for you. If there's a problem, let me know. I'm sure there's a cleaning service we can use."

"We shouldn't have to pay for that." Talbot searched the recesses of her brain for any recollection of Andy Johnson, but she couldn't recall anyone from her past with that name. She honestly didn't want to take the risk of having anyone in her rental who had a connection to her past.

"Andy seemed like a reasonable person and the rent for that place was cheap."

"I can see why," Talbot muttered.

"I'll be there in three or four days. It's all going to work out. Don't stress," Claudia said. "Did you drive past my aunt Georgette's place?"

"Not yet. I'm going to head into town, get some groceries, and I'll snap some pictures and send them your way."

"Perfect. Thanks for doing this. I know you're worried about money and what's next. But we'll be all set once I fix this place up and sell it. Trust me."

"I do with my life," Talbot said. And that was a true statement. While Claudia had taken on a mothering role when Talbot's mother had passed and Corbin had been a toddler, Claudia had become Talbot's best friend. She didn't know what she would have done if it hadn't been for Claudia and her kindness. She'd been there for Talbot when she'd needed a friend and Claudia never left her side.

Talbot couldn't leave Claudia now in her time of need.

Even if that meant being in Candlewood Falls.

"I just texted you Andy's info," Claudia said. "I gotta run."

"I'll see you when you get here." Talbot

tapped the text message and immediately called Andy. It went right to voicemail. She left a message, stating her displeasure and asking for a cleaning service. She set the phone back in her purse. She tucked her hair into a ponytail and placed the big hat on her head. Even though her hair had been much lighter when she moved away and had a little plastic surgery to fix a broken nose and hide some scars, she didn't want to take any chances.

The drive into town didn't take very long. She found a parking spot on Main Street not far from Green Bean.

Memories of her childhood bombarded her mind. Her first kiss with Merlot in the park. Watching her mother take an envelope of cash from Mr. River and board a bus to Chicago, never to see the love of her life again.

She'd tried to forget Merlot, but it was hard to when her son looked exactly like his father.

Same deep blue eyes and big smile. Corbin even developed his father's sense of humor and the same mannerisms.

There had been a handful of men in Talbot's life. She cared deeply for everyone, except she couldn't say she loved them and could never pull them into

Corbin's life. She didn't want her son to get attached to a man she wouldn't marry.

Merlot had her heart.

She stared down the street at the construction in front of a new business—a karate school of some kind.

There were a few other new shops in the center of town, but for the most part, not much had changed in this sleepy little town.

She slipped from the vehicle and made a beeline for the coffeehouse. She shouldn't, but all she could think about were those damn strawberry drinks Merlot's baby sister, Zinny, used to beg them to buy her when Merlot had been tasked to babysit. Talk about a kid with energy.

Zinny was as fiery as her red hair.

A little Weezer.

Or at least that's what everyone called her, but Talbot thought the girl to be sweet, kind, and always had something complementary and intelligent to add to any conversation.

Talbot had accepted her fate but had never forgotten the River family.

She stepped inside and immediately her senses were assaulted with the sweet smells of cinnamon mixed with vanilla and topped off with the rich aroma of brewing coffee. She and Merlot used to meet in town, come to Green Bean and grab a couple of flavored drinks and a few pastries, then go sit in the park and talk for hours. She loved to listen to him discuss the finer points of making wine. He'd get all excited and his face would light up like the night sky dotted with bright stars.

Except for when Rachel, his brother's girlfriend, would show up. What a piece of work that girl had been. Her family traveled in the same circles as Talbot's father, so she had to spend a fair amount of time with Rachel and they never got along. Every once in a while, Talbot would google Merlot and his family. She knew she shouldn't, but she couldn't help herself. She needed to know he'd moved on and lived a happy life.

Learning he'd gotten romantically involved with Rachel had been a real punch in the gut.

But the hardest one had been finding out Merlot had left the family business to become a parole officer. That didn't make sense. He'd never had an interest in criminal justice or the law. The few times he'd worked for his father at the law firm, he'd scoffed at doing anything related to the profession. Last she checked on Merlot, he'd moved back to Candlewood Falls, and his name was listed on the

River Winery website, but his position in the business wasn't clear.

It didn't matter.

She would stay clear of him and his family.

The line to order was ten people deep. Not too bad, considering it could have been out the door.

Reluctantly, she took off her sunglasses, tucked them into their case, and tossed that into her purse. But she kept her big hat on.

The closer she got to the counter, the faster her heart raced. The longer she stayed inside, the more likely she'd encounter someone from her past. So far, she didn't recognize a single soul, but that didn't mean anything.

"Welcome to Green Bean. How can I help you?" a young woman asked.

"I'll take a strawberry frappe and cinnamon roll, warmed please."

"Absolutely. May I have your name?"

"Talbot."

"It will be ready in a few minutes. You can wait down at the end of the counter," the woman said.

Talbot scurried to the other side of the room. A familiar deep laugh filled her ears as a tall gentleman entered the coffeehouse with his arm looped around a gray-haired woman.

Time had changed Carter and Weezer. They had both aged, but Talbot would recognize them anywhere.

Weezer might not have that vibrant reddish-brown hair she used to have, or her flawless complexion, but her stunning blue eyes were just as piercing.

And Carter's hair might have thinned some, and he'd put on a few pounds, but he was still incredibly handsome and had the same smile as Merlot.

As all his boys.

She turned, keeping her back to the entrance. Thank God, there was a back door. She'd go to the courtyard as soon as she picked up her order.

"Talbot," a gentleman called her name and set her drink and snack on the counter.

Quickly, she snagged it and scurried around a couple of tables, keeping her head down. All she had to do was make it outside to the courtyard. She'd find a table, put her sunglasses back on, and mind her own damn business.

"Humph." She hit something—or someone—tall and hard. "Shit." Her strawberry drink spilled down the front of her shirt. It also landed on… she glanced up, adjusting her massive hat.

Merlot.

She blinked, staring into his deep, soulful blue eyes.

"I'm so sorry." He raced to the counter and grabbed a handful of napkins. "I was trying to get my parents' attention and didn't see you." He held out his hand and stared with wide eyes. "You look like someone I used to know."

With a shaky hand, she took the napkins and patted down her chest. "I get that all the time. I think I have that kind of face."

"Let me buy you another one of these." He took her cup and tossed it in the garbage. "My baby sister drinks these all the time. She's totally addicted to them, and come to think of it, the girl you remind me of used to like them too." He lifted the cup. "Hey, Dad. Add a Zinny drink to the order, please."

"That's really not necessary." Shit. Shit. Shit. This was not good. She needed to get the hell out of town. Screw having someone come out and clean the rental. It would give her something to do while she waited for Claudia to come to town.

"I should be buying you a new outfit too," Merlot said.

"It was my fault," she managed to choke out. She reached over her shoulder and took a few strands of hair and twisted them through her fingers.

He stretched out his arm. "I'm Merlot River. My family owns The River Winery outside of town."

Her heart beat so fast she thought it would jump right out of her damn chest. "It's nice to meet you. I'm Talbot Grant."

"Hey, son." Carter River approached holding two drinks on a tray and a bag of goodies. Weezer stood at his side with two more drinks.

"Dad. Mom. This is Talbot. As you can see, I managed to spill her beverage," Merlot said.

"Oh, dear. You're never going to get that out," Weezer said.

"It's a pleasure, Talbot. I'm Carter, and this is my wife, Weezer. Are you new to Candlewood Falls?" Carter asked.

"I'm just passing through." Day one and she'd literally bumped into all the people she couldn't afford to see. She gripped her purse with her free hand and thumbed the strap.

If she got through this and they were none the wiser, she'd make it through the month. However, that meant she needed to go around town and behave like she belonged.

Because she didn't.

This wasn't her town anymore.

And these weren't her people.

"Well, welcome," Weezer said. "Come to The River Winery and I'd love to give you a free bottle of wine as a welcome to our town."

"Thank you. I appreciate that." No need to be rude and tell Weezer she'd never show up. She knew Weezer would take that as a personal insult and there was no reason to piss her off.

"What brings you to our town?" Carter asked.

"I'm helping a friend who recently inherited an old mansion." There were things she had to lie about —like her past identity—but she could be honest about her reason for being in Candlewood Falls. Claudia had no idea about Talbot's connections and wouldn't hesitate to mention her assistant to anyone who asked.

"You must be referring to Georgette's place," Merlot said.

"Yes. My friend, Claudia, is her niece." Talbot nodded.

"Is Claudia here?" Carter asked.

"Not yet, but I expect her in a few days." Talbot glanced at her watch. "I really need to get going. It was nice to meet you all."

"You as well," Merlot said. "I hope to see you at the winery."

Talbot scurried out the back door. She paused,

glancing around at all the people sitting at tables, hiding behind their computers or engaging in deep conversations.

Immediately, she recognized Chablis and Dax. Were they together? Wow. That would be something if they were. She'd seen the image of Dax painted on the brewery building as she came into town.

A hockey star.

He was as handsome as ever and had his hand on Chablis' leg. That's when she noticed a baby carriage on the other side.

She took her sunglasses out and shoved them over her tear-filled eyes. At one time, she felt a part of the River family. They had welcomed her into their home. Their lives. They loved her and offered to help.

And then Carter and Weezer sent her away.

The grown-up Talbot understood it was for the best.

The seventeen-year-old Daisy could never forget or forgive.

She marched around the building toward her car. No reason to chance running into anyone else. Green Bean had been a mistake. While the grocery store could be another place where she could run into people from her past, it would be easier to avoid them.

After today, she'd avoid town at all costs.

No matter how much she wanted to get to know the adult version of Merlot, she couldn't risk him finding out she wasn't just a girl who looked like Daisy.

Merlot

Merlot stared into his half-empty coffee cup. Thoughts of the past swirled in his brain. Guilt filled his heart. The first few years after Daisy died, every decision he made, he wondered what she would have thought. He would spend hours deliberating what to do because he didn't want to disappoint Daisy. When he switched gears in college to criminal justice after Merlot and Chablis had abandoned the family business, he went to Daisy's gravesite and discussed his thoughts with her at length. He explained what happened between Malbec and their mother. He told her what had happened to Caleb and how it personally affected him. Deep in his heart, he believed Daisy understood and would approve.

But as the years passed, so did his connection to his first love. It wasn't that he hadn't thought about her nearly every day, because he had. Something always happened to remind him of the love they once shared. However, it had become easier to move past all the pain, anger, and sadness that had consumed his soul. He'd found a way to live his life.

And be relatively happy.

The only thing that had been missing had been true love.

It wasn't for lack of trying. He'd wanted to settle down and have a family to call his own. He knew that's what Daisy would want because if it had been he who died, he wouldn't want her pining after him all these years. He'd want her life filled with all life could offer.

"What has you so deep in thought?" his mother asked, tapping her freshly polished nails against the table. "Besides your brand-new shirt being ruined."

He glanced at the red stains on the button-down he'd gotten from his little sister for his birthday. "Did you not see the resemblance?" He lifted his gaze.

"What are you talking about?" His father sipped his coffee.

"The woman who spilled the drink all over me." He waved his hand. "Don't you think she looked like Daisy?"

His father leaned back and rubbed his chin. "I don't know, maybe."

"I could see a little in the eyes," his mom said. "But I think you're sensitive to it because of the time of year and the rumors about her father's possible bid for governor."

"He certainly won't have anyone in this family's vote." His father shook his head. "Even if I agreed with his politics, which I don't, he's corrupt as hell."

"Not to mention everything he did to Daisy and her mom." Merlot had dealt with many criminals during his time as a parole officer. Some were remorseful and wanted to change. Others couldn't have cared less and returned to their old ways. Merlot wanted to make a difference after his buddy Caleb had been accused of a crime he hadn't committed.

The justice system was imperfect in so many ways and all Merlot wanted to do was correct it where he could. He wanted to help those incarcerated for all the wrong reasons. Or even those rightfully sent to prison to turn their lives around. He had felt good about his career choice for many years. He believed in what he'd been doing and could see all the good he'd done. His choice to leave the parole department hadn't been an easy one. However, it had been the right time to return to Candlewood Falls and rejoin the family business and his first passion: making wine. Although, he didn't have a degree and he had so much to relearn, but he was up for the task.

"Richard Berkin belongs in prison," Chablis said. "Wouldn't it be nice if he did run and his opponent managed to find all the shitty things he's done while in power as a senator and make that happen?"

"That would be nice, but it won't bring Daisy back." Merlot looked over his shoulder for the beautiful woman named Talbot. It was more than her intoxicating eyes that reminded him of Daisy. In the few moments he'd spent with Talbot, he noticed three things about her that had shocked his system.

Daisy had two nervous habits. She would twirl her hair or hold on to something and stroke it with her fingers. Talbot had done both. Talbot also drank the same thing that Daisy did.

All of those things were common enough. He knew other people who did similar things when nervous and lots of people loved the fruity beverage. Besides, Daisy was dead. Her and her mother's remains had been found in the rubble after a house fire flattened their home. There had been nothing left but singed wood. Everything had burned to the ground. It had been the worst fire this town had seen in years.

His mother reached across the table and rested her hand over his and squeezed. "I wish you wouldn't hang on to the past so much. It prevents you from finding a future."

"You mean a wife," Merlot muttered. Of the seven kids, four were married. Three had kids, and Zinny had officially adopted her husband's son and was pregnant. That left him and his twin brothers for his mom to hassle about weddings. Lately, she'd been relentless in her efforts, especially since Merlot had turned thirty-eight.

"That's not what I said." His mother leaned back and folded her arms. "But you haven't dated anyone in months. You don't seem happy."

"Don't push it, Weezer," his father said.

River, his little nephew, fussed in the stroller.

Dax, his brother-in-law, patted the boy on his back. "I firmly believe in timing and the right person will come along when it's meant to be."

"I agree with that," Chablis said. "However, I do know a girl I used to work with that I'd love to fix you up with."

That was the last thing Merlot needed. "No, thank you," he said. "I don't need a pity date and what about what your husband just said?"

"Hey." Dax lifted his hands. "There's a difference between sitting around waiting for magic and going out there looking for the magic. You can't find the right person without putting yourself out there. What harm can come from going on a double date with us? I've met Chablis' friend. She's a nice girl. If there's no spark, you move on."

"I'll think about it." Over Merlot's dead body would he entertain being fixed up again. The last time one of his siblings set him up, it was a colossal disaster and Pinot Noir didn't speak to him for weeks because of it.

"Whenever you say that, it generally means you're going to avoid answering until it becomes a no," his mother said. "Ever since you moved back to Candlewood Falls, you've been in this weird state of melancholy. It's time to shake that."

His mother wasn't wrong about his emotions. Moving back had brought up things about his childhood that he'd spent a lifetime trying to move past.

He'd carried a part of Daisy with him wherever he went, but he'd done his best to keep her locked inside his heart, where she belonged. She couldn't be the reason he never found a partner to share his life with.

Seeing a woman who reminded him so much of his first love showed him how much Daisy was still part of his thoughts, even if he didn't know it.

"I hate blind dates," Merlot said. "They're always so awkward and uncomfortable. I'd rather find my own."

"Except you don't." Chablis stood. She leaned over and kissed her baby boy, before planting another one on her husband's cheek. "Mom was being kind in her words. I would say you've been downright blue these last few months. The last girlfriend you had I thought was a good match and things were moving along nicely, until River was born, and then it was like you freaked out."

Merlot narrowed his stare. "You're upset because you liked her probably more than I did."

"Yeah, I got attached to the last one, but that's because you made it seem like she could be *the one.*"

"I wouldn't go that far," his father interjected. "I will also add, this conversation is going downhill fast."

Chablis rested her hand on Merlot's shoulder. "If you change your mind, let me know, but for now, Malbec and Eliza Jane are waiting for me at the winery."

"I better head in too." His mother rose with the same grace and style she always did, which tended to make Merlot laugh, but only because his mom was a walking contradiction. Her hair was always styled to perfection and she had a fascination for colored nails and toes. She never missed her weekly appointment at the salon, unless she was sick, and even then she tried to make it in. However, her clothes were often two sizes too big and looked like they were from a hundred years ago. "Don't be late for your meeting with the twins and the new distributor."

"I won't." Merlot gave his mother a hug and a kiss.

"Come on, honey. Walk me and Chablis to work." His mom took his father's hand.

"I better get River home for his nap, or he'll be a beast for the sitter. I'll catch you later." Dax strolled off toward Main Street, leaving Merlot alone with his thoughts.

He checked his watch. The last time he'd visited Daisy at the cemetery had been when he moved back. He'd promised himself and her that he'd make a real effort at restoring family relationships, put his heart back into his career at the winery, and do his best to have a love life in Candlewood Falls.

He could admit that the last one had been a struggle.

It hadn't just been about Daisy, though.

There had been what Rachel had done. If anything, that had soured his desire to be in a relationship. He still distrusted women, thanks to Rachel and her games.

Time to shake off the past. Maybe going out with his sister's friend wouldn't be such a horrible idea.

2

CARTER

Carter sat at the kitchen table with his laptop and cup of coffee. He brought the mug to his lips and sipped. He'd never questioned whether or not he'd done the right thing when it came to Daisy and her mother. Richard would have continued to beat them down until nothing was left, especially regarding Heather. Carter had known for some time what Richard had been doing to his wife and it utterly terrified him that it might have spilled over to Daisy.

His worst fears had materialized the day Merlot had come to him after his girlfriend showed up with a black eye.

What had horrified Carter was that it had been going on for years and Daisy never told a soul.

Not even Merlot.

The poor girl had suffered in silence, all in the name of protecting her mother.

"You're up early." Weezer strolled into the room, freshly showered and ready for the day.

He glanced at his watch. "So are you."

"You tossed and turned all night, which kept me up. Then I smelled that." She pointed to his morning beverage before pouring herself a tall one. She sat across the table and stared out the window as the dark sky gave way to the morning light. "I take it you've been doing a little research."

"You could say that," he said.

"What have you been able to find out so far?"

"Too much and it was too easy." Carter closed his computer and sighed. "I knew where to look, so perhaps that's why I found her so fast. But it's possible Talbot is Daisy."

"That's crazy. Why would she come back here?"

"She gave us her reason and that's because of her boss."

"Georgette's niece?"

Carter nodded.

Weezer tapped her fingers over his laptop. "Tell me what you know about Talbot."

He ran a hand over his face. "I still have much

digging to do and need to check the facts. But here's what I know. Talbot landed in Chicago months after Daisy's supposed death. The story is she moved from California after Talbot's father died in a house fire." Carter arched a brow.

"Jesus, that's a little close to reality. How did you find that out?"

"I called in a favor from someone I went to law school with who practices in Chicago."

Weezer narrowed her eyes. "You reached out to Larry Miller? You know how I feel about that man."

"I agree his ways are slightly unconventional, but he had the connections I needed to get Daisy and her mom underground. While he has no idea what happened to them once I put them on that bus, he does understand how it all works."

"That means you've already had a conversation or two with Larry."

"I called him last night and I got an email from him this morning."

It was rare that Carter kept anything from Weezer these days. He loved her with every fiber of his being and if he left out this whopper of a possibility, not only would Weezer kick him out of the house, but she'd never remarry him, and that was something he wanted more than anything.

"And what did you find out?" Weezer tilted her head and gave him that look that said if he dared to leave one piece of information out, she'd serve his head for Thanksgiving dinner.

"Larry went digging into Talbot's past, but he couldn't find any record of a house fire that claimed her father. We thought maybe Grant could have been a married name, so we looked for a marriage license with Talbot, but found nothing. We decided to change gears and go at it from a different angle."

"Honey, I love you, but can you move this along?"

"Sorry, babe," Carter said. "We decided to go looking for Talbot's mom. Unfortunately, she died from cancer a few years after Talbot moved to Chicago."

"That's rough, to be alone in the world."

"It sure is." Carter sighed. What he was about to say next could go very badly. "But Talbot's not alone."

Weezer was either going to jump up and down for joy or march herself over to wherever Talbot was staying with a loaded shotgun and give that girl a big piece of her mind.

"Does she have siblings?" She blew into her mug and took a sip.

"She has a son," Carter said.

Weezer spit out her coffee. "Don't you dare leave that one hanging. Give me the details." She snagged a napkin and wiped up the table.

"He's almost twenty-one. The timing matches. If Talbot is Daisy, then her son is Merlot's without a doubt."

"There is a chance we have this wrong." Weezer held his gaze. "Just because I got the same feeling you did when looking into her eyes and Merlot saw it too, doesn't mean she's Daisy."

"It could all be one cruel coincidence, but I have to know for sure, not just because we could have another grandchild out there. But I have it on good authority that Richard will announce his bid for governor soon and he plans on doing it right here in Candlewood Falls."

"He questioned the validity of those death certificates. He screamed conspiracy theory and didn't believe his family was dead. The few times he's come back to town, he's made threats that if ever found out that someone put his family up to faking their deaths, they'd rue the day."

Carter had always been on the receiving end of those threats. "My buddies in DC are telling me that Richard plans to make his announcement between now and shortly after the three-legged race. I drew up Georgette's will. I know how long Claudia and Talbot will be in town. It will overlap."

"Maybe we should send Merlot on a trip," Weezer said. "Or at the very least, find a girl and get him good and distracted."

Carter laughed. "You don't mean that. Besides, he's already seen Talbot and we both witnessed what that did to him. If it's Daisy, he's going to figure it out."

"His love for her never died."

"Perhaps that's because his heart knew she was still alive."

Talbot

Talbot groaned when the doorbell rang. She wished she hadn't called the landlord and complained. She had two or three more days before Claudia rolled into town. Cleaning up this rental would give her something constructive to do while she waited. She'd already managed to make the master bedroom and prominent bathroom at least appear clean.

She scurried to the front of the house. A gasp escaped her lips as she stared at Brad Wilde and Lyra Chambers. She cleared her throat. "Um, may I help you?" What on earth would these two be doing at her rental?

And together.

The Lyra she remembered was a total stuck-up snob and wouldn't be caught dead with the likes of someone like Brad.

Not that Brad was a bad apple or anything. Far from it, but they were definitely polar opposites.

"We're here to do a little sterilizing," Lyra said. "I used to live here and I guess Andy never cleaned the place up—or even rented it—after I left."

"I thought he was sending a service." Talbot had been a few years younger than both Brad and Lyra. But she knew Brad well since he'd been close friends with Malbec, Merlot's older brother. This was all too close for comfort. What the hell had she been thinking coming to Candlewood Falls? It didn't matter that it had been twenty-one years.

Or that she was close to thirty pounds heavier.

Had slightly darker hair.

A straight nose and no scars, thanks to an excellent plastic surgeon.

When she looked in the mirror, she could see her old self and Merlot had seen it too.

But Daisy was dead and a remembrance plaque was in the park for her and her mother on a random bench.

"I own the cleaning service," Lyra said. "Unfortunately, it would be ten days before my girls could get you in."

Brad smiled, lifting a big bucket filled with cleaning supplies. "You'll learn that Andy isn't the best landlord. He does almost nothing to keep this place going. I shouldn't be surprised that all the stuff we didn't take with us is still here." Brad peeked his head in the door. "And exactly as we left it. I can't believe he didn't put in new furniture. Half that stuff came from Weezer's basement. I'm so sorry."

"I believe I met Weezer yesterday in town." If Talbot was going to get through the next three weeks, she needed to pretend she didn't know any of these people. It was made easier for her by Brad and Lyra since they didn't seem to be stunned by her resemblance to Daisy. "She seemed interesting."

"That's an understatement," Lyra said. "I still think that woman hates me."

Brad looped his arm around Lyra's shoulders.

"Sweetheart, that is not true. Weezer wouldn't take the time to pick on you if she didn't like you."

Talbot knew that statement to be true.

"Then why does she treat you like you're a king?" Lyra glared. "And me like I'm a stray cat that you picked up on the streets."

"It wasn't always that way." Brad laughed. "Back in high school, she once taught one of the alpacas to chase me and nudge me in the ass. It wasn't funny, but Weezer thought it was hilarious."

Lyra covered her mouth. "I do remember that."

So did Talbot, but she couldn't reminisce with anyone. "That sounds mean," she managed. "I appreciate you both coming over, but I don't expect you to clean. I can do it on my own."

"We honestly don't mind." Lyra glanced up at Brad. "You know, honey, if everything is exactly the same, it's all got to be uncomfortable as hell, especially that mattress. Why don't you see if Caleb, Sam, or someone is around and we can donate some of the stuff we were going to bring down to the mission house."

Talbot swallowed her heartbeat.

Did no one move away from Candlewood Falls?

"That sounds like a perfect plan, but I will make Andy pay for it. Or at least knock something off this nice lady's rent." Brad tilted his head. "I didn't get your name."

"Talbot Grant and please, I don't want you to go to any trouble for me. I'm only in town for three to four weeks. It's not a big deal."

Brad waved his cell. "We're not taking no for an answer." He jogged down the front steps and pressed his phone to his ear.

"May I come in?" Lyra asked.

"Oh. Yes." Talbot stepped to the side. She sucked in a deep breath, letting it out slowly.

Lyra stood in the middle of the family room with a hand covering the center of her chest. "I remember the day I moved in. I'd just come back to Candlewood Falls with my kids after a bad divorce. Life was a struggle then, but everything's changed." She smiled. "What brings you to our quaint little town?"

"The woman I work for is going to be renovating a mansion in town."

Lyra nodded. "Georgette's house. Everyone is talking about this niece she left the place to. We're all curious as to her plans."

"That's not for me to get into," Talbot said. Until Claudia could get inside her aunt's place, there was no plan other than to sell it. But they had no idea what kind of shape it was in, with the exception of the outside, which definitely needed some tender loving care.

Talbot had always had a flair for decorating. While she'd started out in housekeeping at the hotel back in Chicago, she'd moved her way up into hospitality until she finally landed as Claudia's assistant, where she got to flex her muscles with some of the massive parties and banquets.

"Have you made your way into town yet?" Lyra asked.

"I have. It's really delightful."

Knock. Knock.

Brad stepped into the house. "I couldn't get Sam or Caleb, but Merlot and his twin brothers are free. They will be here in ten minutes to help remove all this old furniture, and then we'll go get the stuff we're getting rid of."

Shit. Shit. Triple shit. This was exactly the help Talbot didn't need. "This is too much. I can't ask you to do all this."

"You're not. Andy is and for my trouble, he's knocking a week off your rent. You'll be getting a refund by the end of the day. If you don't, call me, because Andy is known for taking advantage." Brad kissed Lyra on the cheek. "Besides, the stuff we're getting rid of isn't that much better."

"But the mattress is one hundred percent more comfortable than the crap in the main bedroom," Lyra said.

Brad stretched his back. "The few nights I slept here I thought it was going to destroy my spine."

Lyra rolled her eyes. "No need for the dramatics, dear. That's my job."

"And here I thought it was my daughter's job." Brad laughed.

"You have a daughter?" Talbot hadn't meant to ask the question, much less sound so surprised.

"We have an entire brood, but her boys are from a previous marriage and I have a daughter from a past relationship." Brad smiled. "But we make it work."

"Do you have children?" Lyra asked.

If she lied and Claudia mentioned her son, it would make her look like an asshole. But with Merlot heading to the house, the last thing she wanted to do was get into a long discussion about raising children, or the fact her son was an adult and she'd been a teenager when she'd had him.

Ding-dong.

She was literally saved by the bell.

"That must be Merlot and the twins." Brad turned and sauntered toward the door.

"So, you met Weezer. Have you met any of her kids?" Lyra asked, thankfully forgetting all about her previous question.

"I believe it was Merlot who dumped my drink on me yesterday at the coffee place in town."

"Oh, he's so handsome. And single. Are you married? Have a partner?"

"Neither," Talbot admitted. "But I'm not looking."

"I wasn't either when Brad came into my life." Lyra waved her hand. "Is there anything in this house that you really want to keep?"

"I'm not staying long, so I'm honestly not sure why you're going to so much trouble."

Lyra shrugged. "Paying it forward."

"That's real kind of you." When Talbot first moved away from Candlewood Falls, the thing she missed the most was the kindness and generosity of the people. While she'd made many new friends, the city itself didn't have the same small-town feel. It had been overwhelming, especially after her mother had died. If it hadn't been for Claudia, Talbot would have been lost. Becoming a mom at eighteen had been hard enough, but to do it without support would have been impossible.

"After they move the furniture out, I'll start cleaning."

"I insist on helping," Talbot said.

"I won't say no to that." Lyra glanced over her shoulder. "Here they come."

Talbot pressed her hand over her chest, mentally preparing herself to see Merlot again.

It was going to be a long afternoon.

Merlot

Merlot said goodbye to his brothers and Brad and Lyra. He had no good reason to give for staying behind, other than there was still one room left to be deep cleaned, and he intended on seeing this project through.

Not because he enjoyed cleaning. He hated it. That's why he borrowed his brother's housekeeper twice a month. His family teased the crap out of him, considering he lived in the cottage at the winery, and it was only at best nine hundred square feet.

"Here you go." Talbot handed him a beer.

"Thanks." He took a seat on the front porch. "I'll finish this and then help you with the guest room."

"You don't have to. You and your friends have done more than enough. I can handle the rest of this on my own." She eased down on the step, stretching out her legs and crossing her ankles.

All day he'd been unable to keep his eyes off Talbot. She had a sweetness to her that called to his heart. But there was also an edge to her personality that told him she'd been through some things.

He also found himself looking at Talbot's physical details.

It was crazy. This person wasn't Daisy. Yet, he wanted to find that one thing that would prove what his heart so desperately needed to believe.

"I've got nothing else going on today." Slowly, he sipped his beer, savoring every drop because as soon as it was gone, he had no excuse for being a slacker.

"Don't you have a job?"

Merlot chuckled. "I work for the family business. While my mom keeps telling me that I'm going to be the one in her shoes with Zinny at my side, my role is more undetermined at the moment."

"How can that be?"

"It's an incredibly convoluted long tale, but I'm

happy to tell you if you want to hear it." He lifted his bottle.

"Sure. Why not."

"I originally went to college to become a viticulturist and vintner, like my mom, older brother, and sister. But thanks to a family feud and decades-old secret, Malbec and Chablis quit my sophomore year. I decided if they weren't doing it, neither was I. So, I became a parole officer until last year."

"That's quite a career switch." Talbot lifted her drink to her plump lips. "Why?"

"Malbec had a buddy who got a raw deal. I had an ex-girlfriend who screwed me and my brother over."

Talbot jerked her head.

"That's a long and gross story, but in a nutshell, I ended up going out with my brother's ex and it turned out to be hands down the worst decision of my life."

"What made you decide to return to the winery?"

"When my brother and sister came back, I wanted to do so as well. I also missed the wine business. The only problem is all the training I had as a teenager is dated. I have to relearn how to make wine and grow grapes." He lifted his finger. "But Malbec's wife is also a talented vintner and there is something to be said for too many cooks in the kitchen. I also don't have the same passion as they do and my dad has it in his head that I have better management skills than anyone in the family."

"What does all of that mean?"

"I spend some days learning new processes. Going over blends with Malbec and his wife. Or checking on the grapes with Chablis and my mom. Other days I help out my baby sister in the office with the books. I give tours. I do tastings and pairings. I do classes. I run the gift shop. Help make decisions on what we carry or which vendors we will work with. Whatever my mom tells me to and when I told her this morning that you needed help, she gave me the day off."

"Just like that." Talbot snapped her fingers. "She let you go spend the day moving furniture for a stranger."

"It was Brad who called and my mother adores that man as if he were family. She also has an odd affection for Lyra ever since she moved back into town."

Talbot covered her mouth, shutting down a laugh.

Merlot enjoyed the sound of Talbot's voice and the way it slid over his eardrums and landed in his brain like a warm blanket. If his memory was correct, it differed slightly from Daisy's.

He'd spent the day searching for similarities. He'd found a few. The way she tilted her head or toyed with her hair. But so many people did those things. However, three things reminded him he couldn't bring anyone back from the dead.

Daisy had a scar on the side of her face from her father's ring and on her hip from when she'd fallen off her bike as a small kid.

And then there was her nose, which her father had broken, making it visibly crooked.

Talbot had none of those things.

"What's so funny about that statement?" Merlot asked.

"Lyra mentioned that she thinks Weezer hates her."

"That's because Lyra is afraid of my mom." Merlot examined his beer before taking another slow sip. He was at the halfway mark. Maybe he'd ask for a second. "Anyone who acts that way with my mother gets her *angry, I don't like you* side. Deep down, my mom is the kindest, sweetest woman there is. She'll lay down her life for you when you have her as a friend. But she enjoys messing with you."

"Sounds like she was an interesting mom."

"That's an understatement." Merlot moved from his chair to the step to be closer to Talbot.

He felt a pull to this woman he hadn't felt in years. There had been a couple of girls he dated who had taken hold of his heart, but none of them gave him a sense of being grounded. That feeling of being home.

Sitting on this front porch with Talbot, drinking a beer, looking out at the sun lowering in the sky, gave him this warm tingle in his skin that this is where he belonged. It wasn't just his surroundings that sucked him in, but Talbot as well. "This piece of property is amazing," Merlot said.

She glanced over her shoulder. "I don't know about that. The house is run down and needs a lot of work."

"If I owned it, I'd tear it down and build a new one."

"That would require a lot of money."

"I've spent my entire adult life living off almost nothing. I rented tiny apartments and put most of my paycheck in the bank." He chuckled. "I'm currently living on my parents' winery in a little cottage rent free. I've never been one to spend money. With a little help from the bank, I bet I could swing it."

"I wish I could say that. I've always lived at a hotel. Our rooms were cheap and while I'm not into designer clothes and shoes like my boss, I do kind of have a thing for expensive handbags."

"Everyone has a vice."

"Yeah. What's yours?" She dropped her feet to the step, rested her elbows on her knees, and cradled her cheeks in her hands.

"I'm a walking contradiction." He set his beer aside and leaned back. "A career as a parole officer tends to make you distrusting. Everyone I worked with were criminals and I'd say more than half of them made a habit of lying to me. I learned not to believe a word that came out of their mouths. However, I always wanted to believe them. I want to trust people, but I don't. It's a weird conundrum to walk around in."

"That sounds like you feel that way about people in general, and not just those parolees you were charged with."

He laughed. "I've had that problem since I was twenty, before I started my career."

"What happened that made you so distrusting?"

Merlot never liked talking about his past, especially regarding Rachel, but she'd gotten what she deserved. His father had made sure she felt the pain of her false accusations. Merlot hadn't cared about the slander or the civil suit. What mattered more to him was the public apology. However, that never came. She negotiated the civil suit and paid the restitution when they settled it.

And then they both signed a nondisclosure agreement.

He could only say so much.

"It's been a series of events starting with family secrets, dating the wrong woman who used a personal tragedy to gaslight me, then tried to destroy my character years later, to constantly holding everyone to a standard that I'm not sure exists, but believe died with my first and only love." Whenever anyone asked him about his past, or he got into in-depth conversations with a woman he'd started dating, he rarely discussed Daisy. He didn't feel the need to share that the love of his life had died when he'd been only seventeen. It wasn't about keeping it a secret, but more about protecting her memory. At least that's what he told himself.

His family had a different theory. They all believed he didn't share anything about Daisy because if he did, it would free him from the chain he'd attached to her death.

It made sense, considering there was a sense of freedom sitting on this porch and expressing a small portion of his feelings.

"That's a lot." Talbot sat up taller. "I'm stuck on the last part about your first and only love dying. Do you mind if I ask what happened?"

"That might require another beer." His chest tightened. A part of him felt as though Daisy were present somehow. That her arms were stretching down from heaven and wrapping around his body, telling him it was all okay. It was odd because he'd never felt this close to Daisy before. It wasn't that he didn't believe he carried her with him; it was just that this was the first time he could sense her presence.

"I think I can handle that." Talbot jumped to her feet and scurried off inside.

He glanced over his shoulder and groaned. It had been a long time since a woman made him feel this alive. He did worry that her resemblance to Daisy might be part of the attraction, but other ladies he dated had a similar look. He did have a type.

Long hair.

Blue eyes.

Athletic build.

Those were the physical attributes.

Regarding personality, he always enjoyed someone who liked to be outdoors and had a great sense of humor. He wanted someone who could challenge him intellectually, but wouldn't allow him to take everything so seriously.

He wasn't sure where Talbot fell yet, except he enjoyed her company more than any other woman he'd met in a long time.

She returned, balancing a tray of cheese, meats, and crackers on one hand, and carrying his beer in the other. "I thought you might be hungry."

"I kind of am." He nodded.

Sitting cross-legged on the floor, she lowered her chin. "I'm all ears."

"All right, but you must tell me something personal about yourself. Deal?"

"That's fair." She nodded. "You go first."

He took a big swig of his cold brew. It felt good going down. "It seems strange to say this out loud, because there have been other times in my life where I thought I could be in love, but now when I look back on those relationships, I wasn't." He took a cracker and loaded it up with some cheese and pepperoni. He took his time collecting his thoughts.

Daisy deserved to have her memory respected and handled with care. He swallowed and cleared his throat. "The only person I ever loved was my first girlfriend. Sadly, she died in house fire when we were only seventeen."

Talbot reached for the necklace that dangled from her neck. She thumbed the silver pendant. "That's such a sad story. I'm sorry for your loss."

"Most people thought we were too young and couldn't understand what love was, including her father." Merlot smiled. "But my family knew it was the real deal and they were there for me when she died. They wish I would find the right woman and settle down."

"Why haven't you?"

He shrugged. "My sister Chablis believes it's because I'm too picky. My other sister Riesling thinks it all has to do with not trusting. And my baby sister Zinny one hundred percent says I self-sabotage my relationships."

"Do you think any of them could be right?"

"There's nothing wrong with having standards." He laughed. "And the rest, I suppose there's some truth to it. But I also think I haven't met the right person yet."

"Me neither." She smiled. "I also hate dating.

Every time I go on one, especially the first date, it feels like a marriage interview and it's always so awkward. I hate it. But then after the first few times you go out with someone, they always show their true colors, and it's usually nothing like what they said they were like on that first date."

Merlot burst out laughing. "That is so true." He held her gaze, wishing this evening would never end. "Your turn."

"The hardest thing I've ever had to face was watching my mother die." She swiped at her cheeks. "She was diagnosed with cancer and a few months later she was gone. She died in my arms and her last words were: *always remember the love in your heart*."

"Shit. I'm so sorry." He scooted closer, taking her hand. "How old were you when she passed?"

"Right before my twenty-first birthday."

"What about your dad?"

"I lost him when I was a teenager," she said.

"I can't imagine what that must have been like. Losing anyone is hard enough, but that experience has to have shaped everything you've done moving forward."

"It has." She nodded. "But it's made me stronger and I know my mom especially wouldn't want her death to be what defines me."

"I think Daisy—that was my high school sweet-heart—would feel the same way."

"I'm sure she would," Talbot said. "It's important for the living to go on. The only way to honor those who have died is to be the best versions of ourselves and not to let their loss control our happiness."

"Spoken like someone who understands." He polished off his beer. "You're a wise woman, Talbot."

"Thank you for all your help today, but I can do the rest myself. Really. It's getting late and I'm sure you have better things to do."

He helped her to her feet. "Are you sure?"

"I'm tired. I'd rather wait until tomorrow to do it anyway."

"Sounds reasonable." He squeezed her hand. "If you need anything, please don't hesitate to call me."

"I won't."

He really shouldn't be thinking about spending his free time with Talbot. His sister had someone she wanted to fix him up with who probably didn't have any resemblance to Daisy. Add in the fact that Talbot was only staying in town for less than a month, the other girl would be the safer bet.

And Merlot didn't take risks.

"Do you have plans this weekend?" he asked.

"My boss will be here, so it all depends on what she needs me to do."

He would never hear the end of this from his family, if Talbot said yes. "If you're free, would you like to attend a private wine event at my family's winery? We're celebrating a new blend that my sister-in-law created. It's family and a few close friends, but I can bring a guest."

"Oh no." She shook her head. "I wouldn't want to crash an intimate gathering."

"You wouldn't be. Consider yourself personally invited. I'll text you the details. I'm not going to take no for an answer." He brought the back of her hand to his lips. "I'll be in touch."

"I can't commit to anything. My boss will prob-ably have me doing stuff at her aunt's place."

"I'm sure she'll give you a few hours and I can extend an invite to her as well." He turned, jogging down the steps. Excitement bubbled in his veins. This was exactly what he needed.

3

TALBOT

Talbot wrapped her arms around Claudia. "What is so important that it couldn't wait until tomorrow?"

"I have some bad news." Claudia sighed. She took a step back. Her high heels clicked on the hardwood.

"Regarding your meeting with the lawyer?"

"I just got back from his office and it's not good." Claudia took Talbot by the hand and guided her through the old mansion. Talk about a place that needed remodeling. "I've got some lemonade and cookies waiting for us outside by the garden."

Talbot stepped outside into the New Jersey summer heat. It wasn't much different than the weather in Chicago and Talbot loved it. She had always enjoyed the change in seasons. When she and her mother boarded that bus all those years ago, one of her biggest fears was that she'd end up in some southern state where all she'd have was sunshine.

"Who's the hottie working in the gardens?" Talbot took a seat across from her friend. The man looked familiar, but she couldn't tell from this distance.

"That's Silas Wilde. He's part of my news." Claudia crossed her legs, wiggling her foot with her colorful pump. "I'm not used to that big hat of yours."

Silas. Shit. One more person who might recognize her and she didn't need that. "Oh, I'm working on a new look." Talbot had never considered her life a lie, not even when her son asked about his father. She'd done what she had to in order to survive. However, being back in Candlewood Falls, everything felt different, including the things she had to keep from the one person who had been by her side through some of the most challenging times. "Don't you like it?"

"I've just never seen you wear hats before, but it looks good on you." Claudia lifted her drink and took a long chug. "I never did ask. How has this town been treating you?"

"The people are nice." That was a true statement and not because she had a long history with the people of Candlewood Falls. She based her answer solely on her recent experience. "My immediate neighbors came over, helped me clean up, and even brought over some new furniture."

"Why would they do that?"

"Turns out they have a lot of experience with the owner," Talbot said. "Who is a bit of an asshole, but that's all been taken care of and it's just a place to rest my head. I'll be spending all my days over here helping you."

"Unfortunately, that won't be the case." Claudia glanced over her shoulder. "That lawyer I met with this morning, Carter River, he informed me that my aunt put me on a timeline to renovate and I have to do it myself."

"What? That sounds ridiculous." Talbot picked at her fingernails.

"I know. But it's made worse because Silas over there has to plan some garden party. It's all some competitive thing."

"What the hell does that mean?"

"My aunt decided that in order for me to get the money and the house, I have to do everything myself. You might be able to advise me, but you can't lift a finger." Claudia shook her head. "If I fail, I lose everything and Silas is awarded the mansion. I'm not going to let that happen."

"You can't do this alone. It sounds like you got the raw end of that deal."

"I can hire a construction crew, but Carter made it clear, I can't bring in anyone else and that includes you."

Talbot wished she could give her friend insight into everyone in the town. She knew who to avoid, and who would be the better companies to hire. Or at the very least, the right contacts to seek out. But if she did that, she'd have to explain to Claudia how she possessed that knowledge. No way could Talbot risk her identity. She'd seen on the news that her father, the senator, was considering making a run for governor. She couldn't afford for her dad to find out she was still alive.

Or that he had a grandson.

Corbin still had so many questions about his heritage. Telling her son that his father had not wanted him had been the most brutal lie and the guilt she carried weighed heavily on her heart. Corbin had begged her so many times for a name and she refused her son. That had caused a rift in their relationship for a long time.

She had explained to Claudia that Corbin's father was young, like her, and had parents who didn't like Talbot. They had done everything in their power to make sure they tore them apart. When she found out she was pregnant, the father had made it clear his parents had won and he wanted nothing to do with her or the baby.

Eventually, Corbin accepted her answers, but it came up every year around his birthday.

"This sucks." Talbot leaned back and sighed. "What the hell am I supposed to do now?"

"Enjoy a vacation," Claudia said. "Relax a little. Read a book. Check out the town. Once I list this house, our money problems will all be over."

"You know I hate sitting idle, especially since Corbin joined the Army and is now deployed more than he is Stateside. Besides, we need to figure out what's next. I need employment. I don't have a ton of money saved."

"I'm going do everything my aunt put in that damn will and ensure we come out on top. I'll sell this place and we'll move on to the next job. We can start looking. If you find something, I won't be insulted."

The last thing Talbot wanted to do was hang around this town and do nothing. Merlot had texted her twice since he'd been at her house two days ago, asking if she was free for dinner or drinks. He wanted to be neighborly, but she'd told him she would be too busy to do anything but help Claudia with the remodel.

"Trust me, I'm just as frustrated about this as you are," Claudia said. "But if I want to sell this place, I have to play by the rules Aunt Georgette laid out in her will."

"I wouldn't want you to jeopardize that." Talbot lowered her glasses. Silas had aged over the years but was still as handsome as ever. He'd always been kind to her and her mother. However, he had a reputation for being an odd duck. That had been given to him by people who didn't know him well. He was similar to Weezer in that sense. "I'm here to support you in any way I can, even if that means sitting on the sidelines."

"Carter River invited me to some private event at the winery. He mentioned that his son had invited you. I won't be able to go, but you should. I think it would be good for you to do some socializing. You've always been so dedicated to me and to work. Take this time to enjoy yourself."

Shit. If only Claudia knew the truth, she wouldn't be saying that.

"It sounded like a family thing. I'd feel weird going."

"Nonsense." Claudia lifted her cell. "If you don't accept the invite, I'll text Carter for you."

"Don't you dare."

Claudia tilted her head. "Come on. When did you last go to a party or go out on a date?"

Talbot let out a dry laugh. "Seriously. The last man I was involved with turned out to be an asshole."

Claudia cringed. "Okay. You have me there. But I want you to go. Maybe you can gain some insight into Silas and what I need to do to ensure I finish in three weeks."

If Talbot said no, she'd have to give a valid reason and she couldn't come up with one. "Fine. I'll go."

"Good." Claudia smiled. "Promise me you'll try to enjoy yourself."

"I'm not going to approach this as a party, but as a business meeting."

"Nope," Claudia said. "Your job is to drape your arm on Carter's son, smile, and listen. Learn what you can about the people of this town and how I can use it to get a leg up over that man over there."

The one thing Talbot had learned in the last few days had been that not much had changed in Candlewood Falls. Not the vibe of the town and not the people. She didn't have to attend Merlot's wine tasting to give Claudia inside information. But she did have to play along and that's exactly what she'd do.

At least she knew that no one knew who she was, including Carter and Weezer, and they were the only ones who knew that Daisy didn't perish in that house fire.

"I'll do what I can." Talbot owed so much to Claudia and she wouldn't let her down.

Claudia glanced at her watch. "I hate to do this to you, but I've got a million and one things to do."

Talbot rose and gave Claudia a big hug. "Call me if you need anything at all."

"You do the same."

Talbot strolled around the side of the mansion, taking in the property. She'd seen the inside and had no idea how Claudia would pull off the renovation by herself. It felt like a lose-lose situation. Talbot needed to do whatever she could to help her friend. Both Claudia and Talbot needed to beat Silas. They needed to win the mansion, sell it, get the money, and move on. Without it, they would both be in financial trouble.

She climbed into her vehicle, tossing her purse to the passenger seat. She dug into it and pulled out her cell, staring at the last message from Merlot asking her if she'd changed her mind. She hadn't responded to it and contemplated whether it would be wise to stop by the winery.

So far, she'd only had a close run-in with Merlot's parents and the twins. She'd seen Chablis and Dax on her first day, but luckily, she'd been able to keep a low profile. However, the pull to see the rest of his family had been strong. "I'm going because I want a bottle of wine." She pressed the start button and backed out of the long driveway. Her heart beat so fast she almost turned around and headed back to her rental, but the pull to see Merlot again was stronger than all her fears.

Merlot

Merlot climbed the staircase from the gift shop up toward his mother's office, which his little sister, Zinny, currently occupied.

He loved almost every aspect of being back at the winery working side by side with all of his siblings, except Riesling. She'd was the only one who had never had a desire to work at the winery. She'd always wanted to be in the medical field, where she'd stay. The twins had recently quit their jobs with the liquor company to manage the distribution of wines for the family. Things were precisely where his mother had wanted them all along. She had all her kids back living in Candlewood Falls. She had grand-children.

Best of all, his dad was back living in the family home and talking about remarrying his mom.

Life was good.

However, Merlot still felt unsettled. It wasn't because he hadn't mastered winemaking and his skill set was still lacking. He'd get there and he was fine to take things slowly. Understanding the process from grape growing, to putting a bottle of wine into a customer's hand was important. However, it wasn't going to be his purpose in the family busi-ness. He needed to know it because he'd be the man overseeing everything. But Merlot wanted more than a career.

He wanted a family to share it with, and meeting Talbot had reminded him how much his heart ached for a partner.

Leaning against the doorjamb, he tapped his knuckles against the wood. "Hey, Zinny."

She glanced over her shoulder. "What's going on?" She lifted her ginger ale and sipped from the straw.

He handed Zinny a stack of papers he'd tucked under his arm. "I finished the inventory of the gift shop. I thought you'd like it before the end of the day."

"Thanks." She placed it on the desk before taking a cracker and plopping it into her mouth. "My sisters and Eliza Jane warned me morning sickness could be a bitch, but I didn't expect it to be all damn day."

"I thought that was only supposed to last the first three months. Aren't you like five months now?"

"Closer to six. But the doctor said it could last the entire pregnancy with some women, and Mom told me she was always sick with the twins."

"I remember that." Merlot nodded. "She was an absolute bear, but she wasn't any better with you."

"That doesn't make me feel better."

"Just don't lose sight of the fact that you and Toby will have a beautiful little baby in a few months. It's all going to be worth it."

Zinny waggled her finger. "No uterus. No opinion."

Merlot laughed. "Toby mentioned this morning you've been more ornery than usual."

"I forgot you had breakfast with my husband."

"Pinot Noir and Nebbiolo joined us."

"Those two are making me crazy," Zinny said. "They don't get that we do things differently from the way the company we used to work for did. I've tried explaining it to them, but they constantly give me attitude."

"It's been adjustment for them. We're a small winery and they're used to a large distributor."

Zinny rested her hand on her baby bump. "They're making my job incredibly difficult."

"I'll speak to them before I head home this afternoon."

"I'd really appreciate that because Mom won't do it and they won't listen to me." Zinny rubbed her stomach.

"Maybe we should both do it since Mom has it in her head that you and I are going to manage this winery when she retires."

"Doesn't it bother you that you're bouncing around with no real job title and you were always groomed to make wine with Malbec and Chablis?"

Merlot closed the gap and leaned against the desk. "Not at all. First, my degree is in criminal justice. I lost touch with winemaking a long time ago. Besides, I think you and I work well together and the more we expand, the more we will need to rely on each other. The twins will always be salesmen and they're good at it. I have no desire to do that job and I don't think you want it anymore."

"God, no."

"But you did it for a couple of years and understand it where I have more than a working knowledge of growing grapes and what goes into making blends. This way, we can manage all aspects and leave a legacy for the next generation."

"Would you like to feel your little niece or nephew kicking?" She reached for his hand and placed it over her stomach.

"Holy crap. That's one healthy little kid." Merlot had felt a baby kick before and it had always amazed him. But he couldn't believe his baby sister, who was all of twenty-six, was having a kid. He knew without any doubt she'd make for a great mom. She'd already proven that when she'd taken on her husband's teenaged son and adopted TJ.

Zinny had their mother's personality, both good and bad, but mostly all the great parts.

"Tell me about it. He or she does a tap dance on my bladder every day."

"I was surprised to hear you and Toby have no desire to find out what you're having."

"Mom is already putting in her bids for names. Toby and I are not naming this kid after a wine. It will be easier to keep our name choices to ourselves if Mom and Dad don't know what we have until I give birth."

"Taking a page from Chablis' book, I see."

Zinny sighed. "River is a great name for a boy. But we are considering naming this kid after Dad." She waved her finger. "But don't you dare tell anyone or I'll hurt you."

He laughed. "I won't say a word."

The sound of the bell ringing signaled that a customer had entered the store caught Merlot's attention.

"I best get back downstairs. I'm the only one in the gift shop until Bethany returns from her break." He kissed his sister's cheek and headed down the steps, pausing in the middle of the staircase. "Talbot?" He blinked, shocked to see the woman who had been consuming his thoughts for the last couple of days. He'd tried not texting her, but couldn't keep himself from doing it. He desperately wanted to take her to his family's wine tasting. The private revealing of Eliza Jane's new wine was a big deal and he wanted to share it with someone special.

Not a random blind date his sister Chablis set him up on.

She lifted her hand and wiggled her fingers. "Hi."

Playing it as cool as he could, he strolled down the last few steps and met her in the middle of the store. "Welcome to The River Winery. I'm so glad you stopped by. What can I interest you in?"

"I'd definitely like a bottle of red," she said. "I also heard you have cheese pairings to go with your wines."

"I'm happy to help you with that." He smiled. "I'm partial to my namesake, but we have lots of reds to choose from."

Her cheeks turned a pretty shade of red. "Since you mentioned it, I'll try your signature Merlot."

"Good choice. And I have just the cheese platter for you." He lowered his chin. "Are you having a party? Or is this just for you?"

"Sadly, I'll be drinking alone tonight."

"I must admit, I'm a little happy you're not sharing this with some man, but I can't let you drink alone. If you don't have plans tonight, why don't you let me give you a private tour."

"I don't want to put you out."

"Trust me, you're not. My only plans were with a frozen pizza."

She covered her mouth and giggled.

It was the sweetest sound he'd ever heard. When he'd first met her, it had reminded him of Daisy, but he'd pushed all those thoughts out of his head.

Talbot wasn't Daisy.

And he fully believed with his entire being Daisy would approve.

"Did I hear a yes?" he asked.

"Aren't you working?"

"My job includes giving tours." He curled his fingers around her forearm. "Do you have anywhere you need to be for the next hour?"

"No, not really."

Bethany strolled into the gift shop from the back door. Her timing was impeccable. "Hey, boss," she said. "I can help finish inventory."

"It's all done." He smiled. "The only thing I need you to do now is finish the gift baskets for the wine tasting."

"Has the guest list been finalized?" Bethany asked.

"It's on the counter." He squeezed Talbot's arm. "You haven't responded to my text about coming to the party. Now would be a good time to say yes."

Talbot nodded. "I'd love to."

"Wonderful. Bethany, please add Talbot Grant to the list as my personal guest."

"Not a problem, boss," Bethany said.

"And stop calling me that." He shook his head. "You know I hate it."

"Your mom said that's why everyone should say it." Bethany tilted her head and gave him a crooked smile. "And she's the big boss. We all do what she tells us. If we don't, she gets ornery."

"My mother isn't here today, so Merlot is just fine." He sighed. He understood his mom believed this would help him gain the respect of the employees, especially when she officially retired. But he thought it was stupid. Everyone knew he and Zinny were in charge when she wasn't around.

"Whatever you say, boss." Bethany turned and disappeared into the back room where they kept the supplies to make the baskets.

"I guess you're the boss around here," Talbot said with a sweet grin as she took off her big hat.

He took it from her and set it behind the counter. He much preferred her without it. He enjoyed being able to see her entire face, but especially her piercing blue eyes. They were big, bright, and full of life. Her gaze sucked him in like a train wreck. Their familiarity terrified him in ways he didn't want to admit. He pushed that feeling to the back of his brain and focused on all the things that were Talbot.

She was beautiful and intelligent. He didn't care that she'd put up a giant wall and was incredibly reserved. There was something intriguing about her that made him want to know every detail about her life.

"Not until my mother actually stops coming in and telling everyone what to do." He looped his arm around Talbot's waist. "Have you been on a wine tour before?"

"I can't say that I have."

"My brother and his wife are in the bottling room. Eliza Jane has a new white wine line. There will be more than this Pinot Grigio that we are revealing at the event, but the others either aren't ready yet or need to age longer. We're calling the line Blue River."

"I understand where River came from because

that's the winery's name. But why Blue?" Talbot asked.

"That's Eliza Jane's maiden name and here's a little fun fact. My family stole this winery decades ago from hers. This big dark secret was handed down from generation to generation until it landed in my mother's lap. She couldn't live with it anymore, so she brought Eliza Jane here to make things right. My brother Malbec fell in love with her and now history has corrected itself."

Talbot held on to his arm as they strolled through the corridor, past one of the tasting rooms. "That's such a sweet story."

"It ended up that way, but let me tell you, it wasn't fun while we were going through it because that secret nearly destroyed this family. My brother left shortly after college and moved to Napa Valley. Chablis ended up becoming a firefighter, leaving the family business as well. I followed, which set a precedent for younger siblings." He paused at the bottling room. "For years my mother tried to keep the secret because that's what she was told to do by her father. It was this weird, gross game and because my mother is a little strange at times, she thought bringing Eliza Jane in and making her head winemaker would solve all the problems. In the end, it did. But we could have lost it all."

"But you didn't."

"Nope, and Malbec and Eliza Jane are ridiculously happy with two little kids." He tapped his knuckles on the door before opening it. "Hey, guys, we've got company." He guided Talbot into the room.

"You're just in time." Malbec held up a bottle. "We cracked one open and are having our own little party."

"You've got to taste… oh. Hi," Eliza Jane hopped off the bench. "Who do we have here?"

"This is Talbot. She's staying in the house Lyra used to rent. She works for the woman who's Georgette's niece," Merlot said.

"It's nice to meet you." Malbec took down two glasses and poured. "I hope you like a good Pinot Grigio. We paired it with some cheese. My wife really outdid herself with this. I bet it fast becomes our best seller. We need to discuss the price because lowering it a couple of dollars would be a good idea. We can produce this one fast, but the rest of the line, we can—"

"I don't think our guest wants to hear us talk shop," Merlot said. "But I agree and I'll bring it up with Zinny and Mom in the morning."

"Don't stop on my account. I find this fascinating." Talbot accepted the glass Malbec offered and took a sip. "Oh, my. This is fantastic. Price it right and people will buy it by the case." She lifted it to her nose. "I don't know much about wine, but working in a hotel and hospitality my entire life, we always looked for decent house wines that customers wouldn't snub their noses at during happy hour. This tastes expensive."

"It's not," Eliza Jane said. "It's meant to be a fifteen-dollar bottle or less."

"The hotel restaurant I used to work at would pick this up in a heartbeat at wholesale." Talbot reached for a chunk of cheese. "It's something that we would have been able to give to our VIP guests or as a gift in our bridal suites without batting an eyelash at those prices and thanks to the taste, we wouldn't be worried that it would go to waste."

Eliza Jane set her glass down and wrapped her arms around Talbot. "Thank you. That's about the kindest thing anyone could have said about my wine."

"Where did you find this girl and can we hire her? Because we hadn't even thought to market it that way. What a brilliant idea," Malbec said.

"The twins haven't worked on this line yet, but I

can certainly float the idea with them," Merlot said. "If Talbot doesn't mind us stealing it."

She raised her free hand. "Not at all. But don't you already mass sell your wines through distributors?"

Merlot let out a dry chuckle. "Remember the story I told you about how we all left the family business for a while?"

Talbot nodded.

"Well, besides almost destroying the family, it nearly killed the winery. My mom couldn't handle it on her own and she didn't hire people to do it for her, so things went downhill. These last couple of years we've been rebuilding." Merlot leaned against the counter and finally took a generous gulp of his sister-in-law's new blend. He'd tasted it before, but it had all been while they were in the process of finding the suitable blends. The moment the liquid hit his tongue, his taste buds went wild. "Damn, Eliza Jane. This shit is delicious. I almost feel bad lowering the price."

"Don't," Malbec said. "The cost analysis is right on the mark. We won't lose money doing it. Trust me."

Merlot nodded. "You know, Nebbiolo and Pinot Noir's biggest complaint is that they don't have enough in our catalog to entice the bigger chains to buy from us. It's all local or people who have been buying for years."

"This wine we can mass produce," Malbec said. "We've got the grapes. The harvest will be excellent. We've been able to expand. We'll have two more whites this year and the reds ready next year. I bet we can get POs based on this collection."

"When will your next white be ready?" Talbot set her glass on the counter. She pulled her hair over her shoulder and twirled it between her fingers.

Merlot desperately wanted to touch her silky hair. Feel it against his skin.

"We have a Sauvignon Blanc ready now in the same line. We're just not revealing it yet," Eliza Jane said. "We thought it would be best to give the public a taste of each one separately. Let them enjoy one and hopefully they will be excited about the next."

"That sounds like a good plan." Talbot nodded. "When is the big public reveal of this one?"

"During the three-legged race." Malbec shook his head. "I hate that thing. Every year my mom makes a big deal about it. She has to win so she can host the Holiday Showcase. It's so dumb and everyone cheats."

"That's a local thing, right?" Talbot asked.

"It is," Eliza Jane said. "But it does draw some out-of-towners."

"Are there booths? Do you sell your wine there?" Talbot asked.

"Of course," Merlot said.

"Why not invite distributors or anyone interested in mass orders. Tell them you will have samples of a new wine that's not on the market yet, but will be coming. They will already have this Pinot Grigio, but everyone likes free things." She pointed to the small sample-size bottles. "Make a list of who you invited and personalize the labels. If they don't show, relabel them and use them for other gifts."

"Where are you currently employed?" Malbec asked. "Because if you want a job, we could use someone like you."

"I appreciate the vote of confidence, but this isn't in my wheelhouse," Talbot said.

"I beg to differ." Merlot smiled. "My twin brothers are great salesmen. They are good at closing big deals, but they have only worked for a major distributor. They are new to a family-owned business and they are young. They also suck at marketing and coming up with these ideas. We could really use someone who has fresh concepts like this one.

Besides, didn't you tell me that you were currently unemployed?"

"That's only temporary. Once Claudia finishes this renovation, we'll be leaving Candlewood Falls," Talbot said.

"And going where?" Malbec asked.

"We're not sure, but Claudia has a line on a job for us." Talbot reached for her drink.

That's when Merlot noticed her hand shook.

"You're here for a month?" Merlot asked.

"Less than three weeks now," Talbot said.

"Work for us while you're here," Eliza Jane suggested. "I'm sure we can come up with the funds to hire you as an independent contractor."

"We'd have to get Mom to sign off on that one." Malbec raised his glass. "But when we tell her all this, I'm sure she'll go for it."

"No. I'm sorry. I can't." Talbot lowered her gaze. She held on to the glass with both hands.

"Why not?" Merlot inched closer. "Will you be too busy helping Claudia?"

"I don't know anything about wines. Or your business. I'm not an expert in marketing. I work in hospitality and I'm an assistant. I just got lucky with an idea that you liked." Talbot raised her chin. "I appreciate the offer, but it wouldn't be a good fit."

"If you change your mind, you know how to find us." Eliza Jane glanced at her watch. "Shit. We have to get home. Our oldest has a doctor's appointment. It was nice meeting you and I hope to see you again."

"She's coming to the wine tasting," Merlot said.

"Good." Malbec polished off his wine and rinsed out the glass. "Feel free to take that bottle home. Merlot can package up the rest of the cheese for you. See you later, little brother."

"Later, old man." Merlot slapped his brother on the shoulder before hugging Eliza Jane. He waited a full minute after they left before he closed the gap between him and Talbot. "I wish you would take us up on the consulting even if it is only temporary. It doesn't matter that this isn't your forte. You've got a keen sense of how to create buzz where we need it most." He took her hand and pressed his lips on her warm skin. His heart dropped to the pit of his stomach. His pulse raced. He gazed into her big blue eyes, taking her chin with his thumb and forefinger. He could feel her hot breath coat his body. He couldn't stand it a second longer. He pressed his mouth over hers in a tender kiss.

Her body stiffened for a brief second before she caved in his touch.

As he deepened the kiss, his body responded in

the most unusual but recognizable way. It was if he'd been catapulted back twenty-one years and landed in the arms of the only person he'd ever truly loved. It stunned and terrified him and yet, he felt utterly at home.

The sound of someone clearing their throat caught his attention. He took a step back.

"Excuse me," his father said.

"Hey, Dad," Merlot said. "What are you doing here?"

"Eliza Jane called and said there was wine. Mom and I wanted a bottle so I came to collect it." His dad smiled. "Hello, Talbot. It's good to see you again."

"I should get going," Talbot said.

"I haven't given you a complete tour yet." Merlot rested his hand on the small of her back.

"I didn't realize how late it was and I have a couple of things I need to do in town. I'll see you later." Talbot raced past his dad and dashed out the door, disappearing into the corridor, turning in the wrong direction.

"Talbot, wait," Merlot called, but she was gone by the time he reached the opening. Of course, she was going to get lost unless she found the back door. "I better go help her."

"She'll manage to find her way," his father said.

"It's a maze back here."

"I came in the back, so the door is ajar. She'll be fine."

Merlot raked a hand through his hair. "It's rude to let her leave like that."

His father cocked a brow.

"Don't give me that look. I'm not sixteen."

His dad laughed. "I vaguely remember catching you in this very room with a bottle of wine that hadn't aged properly, playing kissy face."

"Real funny, Dad." Merlot swallowed. The reality of the present clashing with the past swirled in his gut. He couldn't reconcile his emotions.

Daisy was dead.

Yet he had felt her in that kiss, which made no sense.

He peeked his head out into the hallway. No Talbot. "I hope you didn't scare her off. She finally agreed to come to the wine tasting event."

"Claudia turned down the invitation, so that's surprising."

"Talbot would be coming as my guest. Her boss can't make it." Merlot sighed. "I like this girl and I want to get to know her."

"That's obvious."

Merlot glared. "I'm serious, Dad. I'm excited

about someone for the first time in a long while. Everyone in this family has been on me to date. I find someone I'm interested in and now you're picking on me for it."

His father lifted his hands. "It's not that. But she is only here temporarily. Perhaps you might want to pick a girl who's going to stick around."

"Wait until you hear the marketing ideas she just came up with. Maybe I can get her to want to stay." The only problem with doing that was this intense feeling that he could be replacing his past with someone who reminded him of everything he'd lost.

Something he needed to reconcile before he pursued this any further.

"Great news on the ideas, but you tend to pick women who are either only out to make themselves a River, or they aren't willing to make Candlewood Falls their home. That's a problem and I don't want to see you get hurt again."

"I appreciate the concern. But I'm a grown man, capable of making my own decisions regarding my love life."

"I'm still your father and I will always voice my opinion whether you like it or not. Just be careful," his dad said. "Now, I've got a nice romantic night planned with your mom, so I'll grab that wine and be on my way."

Merlot adored his parents. They always had his best interests at heart. And if he were being completely honest with himself, his father was right.

He did have shitty taste in women.

But this time, his father was wrong.

Talbot was different. Special. Unique. And maybe, *the one.*

4

____

CARTER

There was no way in hell Carter would let this go on a second longer. He knew the truth. Larry had all but confirmed it to the best of his ability. The underground wouldn't—couldn't—give out Daisy's new identity or where she landed, but Larry had worked his magic and found enough information to link Daisy to Talbot.

Carter marched up the porch steps. He glanced at his watch. It was nine in the morning. It wasn't an unreasonable hour to be banging on someone's door. But to do so unannounced could be considered rude. Although, in Candlewood Falls, it wasn't uncommon.

He planted his hands on his hips, did his best to rein in his frustration, and waited.

The door rattled and squeaked.

Talbot stuck her head out. "Oh. Hi, Carter." She tucked her hair behind her ears. "What brings you out here this morning?"

"May I come in?"

"Um, well, I'm kind of busy today."

"It's important," he said.

"It's really not a good time. I've got a bunch of phone calls to make, and then I need to help Claudia with—"

"Claudia can't take help from anyone," Carter said with a little more edge to his voice than he wanted.

"Oh. I know. What I'm working on with her has nothing to do with the renovation but potentially our next employment gig." She held on to the door, keeping it as a barrier.

"If you want to do this with me standing on your front porch, we can." He glanced over his shoulder. Why Andy and whoever his business partner was refused to sell this prime piece of real estate was beyond Carter. It would make for an excellent home for a lovely family, but instead, it sat empty most of the time. "There's no one around, so I have no problem having this discussion right here." Damn, he needed to change his tone. He had no idea if he had the right to be this angry. He was generally a contemplative man. He always listened to both sides before making any judgment. But this situation could easily blow up in Merlot's face, and he couldn't stand to see his boy's heart destroyed again.

It nearly killed Carter the first time.

"Fine." Talbot stepped aside. "I guess this has to do with my ideas. I'm sorry if I overstepped." She turned and made her way to the small family room.

He glanced around. The place looked a lot better than when Lyra had been living here. "Your marketing concepts were spot-on. We're going to implement them. Thank you for that."

"Then what's the problem?"

"You and I can't pretend we don't know." He pointed his finger to himself and then to her. "I know who you are and for the life of me, I can't figure out why the hell you would come back here."

She blinked like a dozen times. Her lips parted. Then she folded her arms and her face hardened. Much like her mother's used to do when anyone confronted her on what was going on in that house. "I don't know what you're talking about."

"There are three people in this town who know the truth. Me. Weezer. And you. So don't stand there and lie to me." He took in a deep calming breath.

"I'm sorry I'm coming off so angry, but this situation is dangerous for many reasons."

Her eyes filled with tears as she stumbled backward onto the sofa. She rested her arm over her face and sobbed.

Shit. He hated it when he made any woman cry. Slowly, he eased himself onto the couch and pulled her to his chest.

She resisted his comfort, but for only a second.

"Let it out," he whispered. "And then we'll talk."

Merlot had a meeting until eleven. He'd then asked if he could have a few hours off. Carter hadn't asked why, but he knew Merlot wanted to see Talbot. He couldn't blame his son for that, especially with the way she left the winery. But what concerned him was that Merlot had already commented on the resemblance. He suspected that kissing Talbot had sparked more of a recognition and it would only be a matter of time before his son put it together.

Carter couldn't allow that to happen.

Even though deep down he really wanted it. If two people on this planet belonged together, it was Talbot and Merlot. Carter could feel their love the second he walked into the bottling room. It had been so palpable he'd wanted to shout her identity from the rooftop.

But if he'd done that, he'd be putting her and her son at risk.

He knew what kind of man Richard was. He would use his power and money to make Talbot's life miserable.

Talbot sat up, wiping her tears away.

"I'm sorry I barked at you," he said softly.

"It's okay. I'd probably do the same if I were in your shoes." She inhaled sharply, letting it out in a big swish. She used to do that all the time when she'd been a teenager and she'd come over to the house after her father had done something horrible and she felt the need to apologize for it. "I didn't want anyone to find out it was me."

"Then why did you come back?" Carter asked.

"I didn't really have a choice."

"I find that hard to believe. You're not a kid anymore."

"You don't understand. The woman I work for has no idea about my past. No one does. I've never breathed a word of it. Trust me, I know the risks. So, when Claudia found out about her aunt's mansion and asked me to come, I couldn't say no."

"Why not?"

"She's like a second mother to me in many ways. She was there for me when my mom died. She took me in. Gave me a job. And when we lost ours with the hotel in Chicago, she told me I could come here, help her with the renovations, and then we'd be set up to do whatever we wanted."

"Only, you can't help her, thanks to Georgette's requirements in her will."

"Yeah, that put a little damper on things." Talbot nodded. "But you see, I couldn't tell Claudia about my connection to this town. I thought I'd be able to hide out, but just my luck. Merlot spills a Zinny drink all down my shirt on my first day here."

"Perhaps going to Green Bean wasn't the brightest of ideas." Carter chuckled. "But this is a small town. You would have run into us eventually."

"That doesn't make any of this easier. Merlot is still as persistent as ever."

"Only when it comes to you." He patted her leg. "He hasn't had much luck with dating over the years and this is the first time he's got that spark. Kissing him was stupid."

"He kissed me."

"You could have stopped him," Carter said. "But I get it. The two of you always had such a strong connection. It's a bond that doesn't break."

"What am I going to do?"

"For starters, you can't go to the wine tasting."

She shook her head like a wet dog. "Claudia is expecting me to go. I can't tell her no. She'll wonder why. Lying doesn't come naturally to me, except my identity. That has become second nature. But being back in this town is making it hard. I have to pretend to her that I don't know anything about Candlewood Falls, or the people here. I'm already avoiding her and doing my best to stay in this house."

He arched a brow. "You drove yourself to the winery and Merlot did notice you went out the back door. I told him I left the door open, but he's not stupid and I'm not trying to be mean. But he can't find out. Not just because of what it will do to him, but your father is going to make a run for governor and I have it on good authority he's going to make that announcement right here in his hometown. I'm trying to protect you both."

"When is my father coming?"

"That I'm not sure of, but we will have some warning before it happens."

"Hopefully, I'll be long gone by then." Talbot shifted. "If I could leave now, I would. But I wouldn't know what to say to Claudia. It would be like lying to you and Weezer as a teenager. I couldn't do it."

"I'm not asking you to leave," he said. "But you

have to stop this with Merlot. It's not going to end well for you or him."

"I know that, but lying to him isn't easy either. It's like I'm stuck in this weird alternate universe somewhere between the past and the present and to be honest, I'm terrified of going to the winery party. Especially as Merlot's guest. He's not going to want to leave my side."

"I'll make sure he's so busy he doesn't have time for you."

"Thank you." She let out a huge sigh.

"I have one more question for you." Carter hadn't been proud of the fact he'd looked into her life, but he'd done so for all the right reasons. Hopefully, she'd see it that way too. "I need to know, for my own sanity, if your son is Merlot's."

She covered her mouth and gasped.

"That's what I thought."

"You poked into my life?" She jumped to her feet. "That's so invasive and I don't appreciate it."

"I'm sure you don't." He rubbed his temples. "Why didn't you tell us you were pregnant? I would have never put you on that bus if I knew that."

"Not that it's any of your business, but I didn't know until about a week later." She let out a sarcastic laugh. "I ran away three times, all with plans on coming back to tell Merlot about the baby. It was so wildly unfair to me, Merlot, and our son."

"Does he have any idea who his father is?"

She kicked the couch. "Are you crazy? Of course not."

"Who does he think his dad is?" Carter had no right to ask, but curiosity got the better of him.

"He has no idea and I plan on keeping it that way. You don't know what it's like to look in my son's eyes every day and tell him that his father didn't want him." She held up her hand. "I know that's not true. If Merlot knew, he would have been the greatest dad ever. And you know what, my son looks exactly like Merlot. It fucking kills me to lie to him like that."

"Now there's the Daisy I know," Carter said. Even though she tended to be a quiet kid, she could have a mouth like a truck driver when she got fired up.

"My name is Talbot. Don't ever call me that again."

"I won't," Carter said. "I'm sorry that things went the way that they did. I wanted so desperately for your mother to leave your dad. I tried helping her. We called the cops and—"

"I got a broken nose." She pointed to her face.

"Which I've since fixed. But my dad had half the sheriff's office in his back pocket. He had money and power and he used it to control my mom. The only way out was to die. I understand that. I know you did the right thing, even though it broke my heart to leave Merlot."

"I broke his too," Carter said. "Not to mention mine and Weezer's. We loved—love you. If I didn't believe your father would do something crazy if he found out you were alive, I'd tell Merlot the truth."

"If he knew, he'd never forgive me when it comes to Corbin." Talbot twisted her hair. "We used to talk about how we'd work at the winery together and have two or three kids. He'd stomp on my grave if he knew that I kept his son from him for nearly twenty-one years. I want him to be in love with the memory of the teenager who died. Not hate me."

"If you believe that, you don't know my son as well as you think." He palmed her cheek. "He will resent me and his mother for sending you away. It won't matter that we didn't know about the baby. It will only matter that it was our idea."

"I'm sorry I put you in this awful position."

"You're just going to have to make it clear to Merlot that there can never be anything between you and him," Carter said. "I'll take care of everything else." He kissed her cheek. "I'm proud of the woman you've become."

"Thank you. That means a lot coming from you," Talbot said. "Please let me know if you hear anything about my father."

"There is one thing you need to know about him." Carter had long debated telling Talbot, but she needed to know what she was up against if Richard ever showed his face in Candlewood Falls while she was still in town.

"What's that?"

"After the fire, your father made a big stink that he didn't believe it was you and your mother who died. I had to pay off a few people at the morgue to ensure the autopsy proved it was. But even then, he cried conspiracy. If your mom hadn't had me change her will to have your bodies cremated, he would have tried to exhume your bodies. I haven't heard him rumble about it for a few years now, but he knew your mom was up to something that last month while I put all that together. He threatened me a few times and came at Merlot as well. If he took one look at you, it would start all over again and all it would take is a DNA sample to prove he was right."

"We have to make sure that never happens."

"Where's your son now?"

"I'm not exactly sure. He's in the Army and currently deployed. Last I heard from him, he's not landing Stateside until next month," she said.

"Does he know where you are?"

"Not yet and I wasn't planning on telling him. We text through an app when he can."

"Keep it that way." Carter squeezed her forearm. "If you need anything or are concerned, call me. Or Weezer."

"I will."

Carter made his way to the front of the house. While he felt better about the situation, he knew his son, and he wasn't going to take a brush-off from Talbot easily.

Talbot

Another tap at the door rattled Talbot's nerves. She'd forgotten about how people in a small town dropped by unannounced. It drove her father nuts when she'd been a kid. He'd been a firm believer that people should call first.

But that had only been because he didn't want anyone catching him beating the crap out of his wife.

Or daughter.

She scurried from the kitchen to the front of the house and pulled open the door.

Merlot.

He stood there with a big smile and her hat.

Well, she was happy about the latter because she wouldn't have to go into town tomorrow for Claudia. While Talbot couldn't help with the renovations, she could do all of Claudia's errands. Usually, she'd be happy to do them, but the idea of running into anyone else who might recognize her made her skin crawl after she met with Carter.

"What are you doing here?" she asked.

"You left this at the winery yesterday."

"It wasn't necessary for you to drive out here and return it. I could have picked it up." Like that was ever going to happen. She would have bought a new one.

"I wanted to talk to you," he said. "May I come in?"

No time like the present to set the proper boundaries. She squared her shoulders. "Sure."

He followed her back to the kitchen, where she

offered him some lemonade. He made himself comfortable at the island.

She opted to keep her distance, leaning against the counter. "What's on your mind?"

"You raced out so fast yesterday after my father barged in on us."

"Yeah. That was a little embarrassing." Her cheeks heated.

"But it was no reason for you to leave. I had been looking forward to spending the evening with you. And why haven't you returned my call or responded to my texts?" He tapped her cell, which she'd left on the counter. "I feel like you're avoiding me."

"I'm sorry. I'm not. I'm just super busy. Claudia is tied up with the renovation, leaving me tasked with finding us employment for when that's done."

"I can't help but wonder if my kissing you has offended you."

It was time to learn how to lie like she never had before. But it wasn't like she didn't know how to blow off a man. She'd gotten good at it over the years. Coming up with excuses for why she couldn't date had become second nature.

When Corbin had been a baby it was easy.

Young men avoided her. Who in their right mind

wanted to take on that responsibility in their early twenties?

But as Corbin aged, men didn't seem to be bothered by her being a single mother. However, her son became her excuse, although it had been her reality. All she wanted to do was be a good mom, and bringing a boyfriend into the mix didn't seem responsible.

The last ten years, she'd tried dating, but she always ended up thinking about Merlot. Even if she found a man she cared for, she felt like she was cheating on the only one she loved.

She'd never been able to forget Merlot. Staring at him now, she understood why. She still loved him, but now maybe she'd have her chance at a last goodbye.

"I promise you, it's not that, but I can't get involved with anyone right now and you just caught me off guard."

"It was a really nice kiss."

Her mouth defied her and she smiled. "I won't deny that. However, I recently broke up with someone and I'm not ready to date. Besides, I'll be leaving soon. It seems counterproductive to get involved with you or anyone."

"Are you always this practical?"

Her son teased her for being so pragmatic. Before he left for his last deployment, he begged her to be more spontaneous. To let her hair down and live a little.

She'd spent her entire life being guarded. First as Daisy, the daughter of a monster. And then as Talbot, an adult who lived a secret identity who was always worried someone would figure out who she really was and go running back to daddy.

Her first few years working under Claudia, anytime a bigwig in politics came through the hotel, Talbot would try to hide and blend into the fabric of her surroundings. Claudia found her shyness endearing.

Little did she know Talbot wasn't shy. It was a trait born out of necessity.

"It's not so much that I'm being practical, but the man I was involved with I loved very much. I'm not over him. I wasn't ready for it to end." She drew on her memories of the Merlot she left behind to tell this tall tale. As if she were telling Merlot about himself. Her heart thumped in the center of her throat. It wasn't a total lie. She wasn't over Merlot. She still loved him, but that didn't change how shitty she felt at the moment.

He took a big gulp of his beverage and leaned

back. "Getting over someone you love isn't easy," he said. "I've been there myself, only she passed away."

"You mentioned that," she whispered. "I'm so very sorry."

"This is probably an inappropriate question, but will you still attend the event at the winery with me?" He held up his hand. "Strictly as friends. I will totally respect your situation and I won't kiss you again."

"I would really love to attend."

"Great." He stood. "I won't keep you any longer. I'm just glad we got to talk."

"Me too." She walked him to the front of the house. "Thanks for returning my hat."

He stood in her front doorway, gripping the handle, staring.

God, she wanted to taste his sweet lips. Feel his arms around her, holding her tight. She'd never forgotten what it was like to be loved by him and she wanted so desperately to experience it again.

"You're not making it easy for me to keep my promise," he murmured. "Especially when you look at me like that." He ran his thumb over her cheek. "Tell me you're not attracted to me and I'll walk right out this door."

"Attraction means nothing."

"And yet it means everything." He inched closer.

She pressed her hand on his chest. She needed to be strong. Allowing her lips to touch his was playing with fire.

"This man, does he still love you? Does he want to be with you?"

"It's complicated," she said.

"How so?"

She opened her mouth, but no words came out. She could say she and this man shared a child, but that would open a fresh can of hell she didn't want to get into, especially with the actual father of her son.

Merlot brushed his lips across hers in quick, but powerful kiss. It wasn't romantic, but it had all the promise of one. "Whoever this man is, he's a fool." He turned and jogged down the porch steps. "See you in a couple of days." He waved his hand over his head.

She closed the door and dropped to the floor, covering her face.

The event at the winery would be the last thing she did in this town. Outside of that, she would hide out in this little house until either she found a job or Claudia was done with her renovation.

Whichever came first.

5

MERLOT

Merlot stood at the front door waiting for Talbot. She'd texted him a half hour ago, stating she was on her way. She should have been at the winery by now. Even if traffic was coming through town, it wouldn't have been that bad.

The sound of a car turning off the main road into the parking lot tickled his ears. He'd been on edge for the last few days, anticipating seeing Talbot again. They'd shared a few lighthearted text messages and one late-night phone call, thanks to half a bottle of wine he'd consumed. No matter how hard he tried, he couldn't get her off his mind. He knew he needed to and maybe when she left town, he'd be able to forget her, but until then, his body knew she was close.

He'd reconciled that he'd never move past the fact she reminded him of Daisy. If things were to get heated between them, he'd have to tell her before it got too heavy. Otherwise, he could only be described as an asshole.

He wouldn't be that guy.

A car parked in the far row. Not wanting to appear too eager, he waited patiently by the door as Talbot strolled through the maze of vehicles. She wore a stunning red sundress with stylish matching heels. Her hair was pulled back into a ponytail at the nape of her neck. She smiled and waved.

His heart fluttered.

"Sorry it took me so long." She smiled. "I had a wardrobe malfunction right before I left. I hope this is okay."

"You look gorgeous." He kissed her cheek. "Dare I ask what you wore before you changed into this?"

"Something a little less flashy." She took the arm he offered. "I much prefer to blend in than stand out."

"You could wear a potato sack and everyone would be staring at you."

"Flattery is not going to get you anywhere," she said.

"I'm only stating the facts." He guided her into

the main room where most wedding receptions were held.

His entire family had already arrived. All of Dax's family had shown up.

So had Raf and Ember. Brad and Lyra. Caleb, Brooklyn, and most of the Wilde family who still lived in Candlewood Falls.

"There you are." His mother scurried to his side. "Hello, Talbot. It's so good to see you again."

"You as well." Talbot nodded.

"I'm sorry to take your escort away, but Zinny needs his help with the baskets. There have been a couple of mix-ups. She's in the back room."

"Can't someone else do that?" Merlot glared.

"It's okay. Go ahead. I know this event is important to the winery and your family. I can manage by myself for a while."

"Are you sure?" Merlot asked.

"Dad can entertain her for a bit." His mom waved to his father, who sauntered over with a big grin.

"I'm a big girl. I'll be fine," Talbot said.

"I won't be long." Merlot squeezed her biceps.

"I'll take good care of her," his father said.

Merlot made a beeline for the staging room where they organized all the gifts and kept extra supplies. He found Zinny and Toby sitting at the table, redoing most of the baskets. "What the hell happened?"

"No idea." Zinny shook her head. "Except they were put together with the wrong bottles and paired wrong. That's not like Bethany."

"Funny thing, Chablis told us she saw Weezer coming out of this room last night." Toby arched a brow. "Could your mom be up to something?"

"Why would she sabotage Eliza Jane's big night? That makes no sense." Zinny playfully smacked her husband's arm.

"Oh, I don't know. Because as much as I've learned to love *the Weezer*, she does some mighty strange things." Toby took a bottle, slapped a new label on it, and placed it in a basket, pushing it toward Zinny, who started filling it with the other gifts.

"So, if the two of you are back here handling this, why am I here?" Merlot scratched the back of his head.

"Because it will go faster and Mom is being weird about me carrying anything over an ounce. Like lifting one of these baskets will harm the baby." Zinny lifted her ginger ale and sipped through the straw.

"You did give me a scare yesterday with contractions." Toby rested his hand on Zinny's shoulder. "The doctor said you needed to rest."

"Wait. What?" Merlot pulled up a chair. "Why am I just hearing about this now?"

"Because you're preoccupied with the new girl in town and I don't want everyone being strange and coddling me. It's bad enough that my mother showed up at my house this morning ordering me to eat breakfast in bed and my husband thinks I should keep my feet up all day. I'm not in labor. I'm just at risk for it happening early."

"Zinny, that's a big deal," Merlot said. Now he understood why Zinny had taken two days off. He didn't question it because his family always covered for each other. There certainly was enough of them to do that, but he hated it when they kept secrets. That's always what got this family in trouble.

"I keep telling her that, but you know your sister. More headstrong than her mother." Toby pushed another basket to the side. "I didn't even want to come tonight. I thought it best to stay home with all our feet up."

"I think that would be wise. I can finish this." Merlot took Zinny's hand.

"The doctor said it would be fine." Zinny smiled. "But I guess now is as good a time as any to tell you that I am going to have to cut my hours and I'm not really supposed to do stairs until this little tyke is born."

"I can handle everything. Don't worry about a thing." Merlot smoothed his hand over his sister's growing belly. "All we want is a healthy baby."

"It's a girl, by the way," Toby said. "But if you tell Weezer, we'll both have your head on a platter. She'll want to name it Syrah or Rose."

Merlot laughed.

"We've settled on Crystal." Zinny wiped a tear from her cheek.

"That's a beautiful name." Merlot hugged his sister. "Go home. Let Toby pamper you for a change."

"When you make the suggestion, it doesn't sound as gross as when Mom says it." Zinny set her beverage on the counter and stood. "I am exhausted and Eliza Jane and Malbec will understand."

"On your way out, send in one of our other siblings to help me." Merlot took his sister's seat and began where she left off.

"Will do." Toby gave him a brotherly squeeze. "Thanks for talking some sense into her."

"Watch your tongue, husband. Or I'll stay." Zinny took Toby by the hand.

He groaned.

Merlot laughed.

Those two were the most unlikely and interesting couple he'd ever met. But they worked.

A few minutes later, Chablis strolled through the door. "I'm so glad you got Zinny to go home. I don't understand why you're the only one she'll listen to."

"Because the rest of you talk to her like she's a child," Merlot said. "I get she's the baby of the family, but she's married with a kid on the way. And let's not forget she adopted Toby's teenage son."

"I haven't forgotten any of that, but she can be such a brat sometimes." Chablis plopped herself down across from Merlot, glanced at the guest list, picked up a label, and smacked it on a bottle.

"She's only reacting to the way you talk to her." Oftentimes, family dynamics got under Merlot's skin, especially this ongoing battle between Chablis and Zinny. He didn't have this problem with Riesling. Of course, his other sister didn't work for the winery and never would. That did make things easier.

"You know, the twins say the same thing about you. They didn't appreciate you telling them how to do their job. Although, I will admit, that girl who has you all hot and bothered has some interesting ideas."

Merlot burst out laughing. "Maybe if Pinot Noir and Nebbiolo got their collective heads out of their ass and realized that we're a small family winery and not a big distributor, they could see that they needed a new approach." He raised his finger. "And I never told them how to do their job. I merely made a suggestion. It's mine and Zinny's job to make sure this place runs smoothly. Yours, Malbec's, and Eliza Jane's is to make the wine and curate the grapes. The twins' job is to sell it. Things are that simple."

"Why are we biting each other's heads off?" Chablis shook her head. "And why the hell did Mom do this? Because I know she did. I saw her scurry her funny little ass out of here with a guilty expression."

"I can't answer the latter, but I can take a stab at the former."

"I'm all ears, little brother."

"You're annoyed with me because I'm enamored with Talbot, who reminds all of us of Daisy, which is unnerving to say the least. You're making me crazy because you're pregnant again and don't want to share the news yet." He arched a brow. "Tell me I'm wrong."

She sighed. "I wasn't trying to get pregnant. It's too soon. I just had River. What am I? Fertile

Myrtle? It's like Dax looks at me and he knocks me up. He's got some serious super sperm."

"That's a little too much information, even for me," Merlot said. "How does Dax feel about this?"

"He's freaked out a little too. We were happy with having one child. I'm freaking forty."

"That's not too old to have a baby."

"It feels like it is and I had so many complications with my delivery of River. And now Zinny could go into early labor. It's just a lot to take in."

"Breathe, big sister. Just breathe," Merlot said.

"Easy for you to say. You don't have a uterus."

"That's what Zinny told me." Merlot shoved another basket aside. They only had a handful left to do, and then he could go find Talbot and enjoy the rest of the evening.

"Did Talbot arrive yet?" Chablis asked.

"She's hanging out with Dad. I don't know if that's good or bad."

"It's better than if she were with Mom."

"That is true."

"And for the record, I'm not angry with you about Talbot. I want to see you find the right girl. If you believe she's it, I'm all for it."

"I don't know." Merlot pushed the last basket aside. "There's something mesmerizing about her and I can't stop thinking about her, but there's a fundamental problem with that."

"Okay. I'm listening."

"You have to promise not to tell anyone and you can't make any judgments. I don't want lectures. I just want my big sister."

"I can do that." She waved her hands. "Promise."

"I got past the fact she looked like Daisy. But when I kissed her, it was like I was kissing my past. It was the weirdest sensation ever. Talk about a freak-out."

"Maybe it's because you put that thought in your head."

"It could be," he admitted. "It's just that she kissed just like Daisy. I know that's strange to say. I was only seventeen and—"

"Stop with the only seventeen part. I fell in love with Dax when I was sixteen. I've loved that man my entire life. It doesn't matter that we spent many years apart. It doesn't change the facts."

"But Talbot isn't Daisy. It's unfair of me to compare Talbot to a dead girl."

"You're right. It is." Chablis reached across the table. "Your brain and your heart are confusing the past and the present. You and I have always been our own worst enemies. We analyze everything and that gets us in trouble. We sometimes react to things when we should let things happen. Why don't you do your best to enjoy Talbot for the woman she is instead of worrying about why she reminds you of things from the past."

"I feel like I'm being cruel."

"Does she know about Daisy?"

"She knows there was someone I loved once who died. But I haven't told her about how she reminds me of her," Merlot said.

"Maybe that's a conversation you need to have. Perhaps you can get past it if you vocalize it to the person it's directed to."

Merlot knew his sister was right. "I will take your advice and talk to her when the time is right."

The door burst open and their frazzled mother came barreling into the room. "Are you two done in here?"

"We are," Merlot said.

"Good. Good." His mother nodded. "I need another fire put out. Since Zinny went home, Chablis, can you help the twins at the wine table? Merlot, I need you to come with me."

"Can't someone else help you? I want to spend some time with my date." He glanced at his watch. "I've left her alone now for forty minutes."

"Talbot's with your father and she's having a grand time. This won't take too long." His mother yanked him right off the stool.

"It better not," he mumbled. When his mom got like this, there was no arguing with her, so he better hop to it so he could get back to the party and the pretty lady in red.

Talbot

Talbot glanced around the room at all the familiar faces. She'd said hello to a dozen people she'd known from childhood and each one had given her a funny look, but no one said a word about how much she looked like dead Daisy.

Thank God for small favors.

"How are you holding up?" Carter handed her a glass of wine. It was her second and if she wasn't careful, she wouldn't be driving home.

"Hanging tough," she said. "I figure if I can hang out for another hour or so, I can call it a night."

"Weezer had Merlot jumping through hoops. You should be able to make your escape soon."

"I can't thank you enough for doing this. It's tough to resist your son's charms."

"I'm sorry this isn't easier for you," Carter said. "I do need to mingle a little bit. You are welcome to hang by my side if you like."

"I nearly slipped up when I saw Brooklyn."

"I did notice that."

"Would it be okay if I stepped outside and walked toward the vineyards?"

"Please, be my guest." Carter patted her shoulder. "If I run into Merlot, what should I tell him?"

"That I went to the ladies' room. Or that the last time you saw me I was conversing with someone. Anything to keep him from looking for me outside."

"I've got your back. No worries." Carter strolled off into the crowd.

She took her wine and scurried off out the side door. She took in a deep breath, enjoying the evening air. It was a warm night. A little humid, but she didn't care. She was lucky that bugs and mosquitos didn't like her much. She made her way down the lighted path that led toward the vineyard. When she'd been a teenager, this had been her safe place. She could come to the winery and all her troubles would vanish instantly.

The River family treated her with kindness.

Not pity.

They provided her with a safe harbor and all the love in the world. Leaving them had been the most challenging thing she'd ever done.

"There you are," Merlot's voice rang out, landing on her ears like hot fudge melting over an ice cream sundae.

She paused, turning slowly.

"What are you doing out here all alone?" he asked as he jogged down the path.

"I wanted some fresh air." That was the truth. "I was also feeling a little out of place in there with all your family and friends."

"I'm sorry my dad ditched you."

"Oh, he didn't. He was actually very kind. Introduced me to everyone. It was honestly overwhelming."

Merlot laughed, taking her free hand. "Come on. The vineyard is gorgeous at night. But watch your step in those heels."

"Maybe we should get back. I'm sure your family wants you in there."

"And risk my mother finding me again and sending me off to go do something? Absolutely not." He snagged her wineglass. "I should have brought a bottle. But we can stop by my place." He pointed in the direction of the cottage. "I live right over there. You can't see it yet, but there's a small house by the river. I've got a bottle of the new wine. We can fill up and keep walking."

"I won't be able to drive if I have more."

"There is such a thing as Uber. Or I know a few pregnant ladies who aren't drinking." He leaned a little closer. "You can always stay with me."

"That's not funny."

"It wasn't meant to be." He pressed his hand on her back. "But I promised I would be a gentleman, so if you did stay, I would keep my hands to myself. I swear."

"I won't be staying," she said firmly. Unfortunately, she let him guide her right to his humble home. Every muscle in her body ignited with the memory of the first time they'd made love.

It had been right here in this very cottage.

They'd been seventeen years old. His brother, Malbec, normally claimed the cottage as his place when he was home from college, but Merlot used it when he was gone. Their first time had been amazing. It wasn't at all like she worried it would be. Some of her friends told her it would be awkward and it would hurt.

But Merlot had been sweet and tender. When the

pain did come, he did everything he could to ease the discomfort.

And it worked.

She loved him for it.

They had made love five times before she had been sent away, and during one of those times, they had created Corbin.

A name Merlot had picked out one night when they'd been discussing how he'd never name his children after wines.

She had to agree.

When she asked why Corbin, his simply responded it had a nice ring when matched with River.

She couldn't give Corbin the name River, but Corbin Marcus Grant was good enough.

"This is quaint," she said, entering the familiar space. Not much had changed. The pictures on the walls were the same. The furniture was the same, but the comforter was different. So were some of the knickknacks.

"Eliza Jane lived here when she first moved to town. Then Chablis and now me. Eventually, I'd like to buy some land outside of town and build a house, but that will come in time." He set the wineglass on the counter. "I know I said I wouldn't kiss you, but I want to."

She swallowed. Hard.

He inched closer. "You're an irresistible woman, Talbot. I'm drawn to you."

"We shouldn't." She needed to get out of the cottage. Being in this place—with Merlot—was more than dangerous.

"I can't think of one good reason why not."

Her knees buckled as she caved to his sweet kiss. She wrapped her arms tight around his strong shoulders. She couldn't get close enough. Feel enough. She needed him more than she'd ever needed anyone in her life. She was desperate to feel all of him again. To be a part of him.

He pulled back, palming her face, and smiled.

"Kisses sweeter than wine," she whispered. The phrase tumbled from her lips. She wished she could take the words back, but it was too late. The damage was done and there was no turning back now.

He stared at her with his mouth open and questioning eyes.

The spark of recognition was written all over his face.

He'd uttered those exact words after their very first kiss and the first time they'd made love. It had all been so magical. Like it had been a fairy tale. If she didn't have Corbin, it could have all been a fantasy.

But it had been real.

She wanted to run and hide, but her body froze.

"How did you know to say that to me?" He dropped his hand and narrowed his stare. A look of anger and confusion filled his deep soulful eyes. "Where do you know it from?"

"Isn't a song or something?" she said with a quiver in her voice.

"Those words mean something deeply personal to me and you couldn't have randomly picked them out of a hat. How do you know them? Tell me." His gaze bored right through her like a spotlight shining on all her lies. "Don't lie to me."

Tears burned her cheeks. She couldn't stand it a second longer. She needed to get the truth out or it would eat her alive. "You said it to me under the bleachers at school," she choked out. "And then again right here after you made love to me for the first time."

He took a giant step back. "How is it you? How is this possible? And why the hell have you been lying to me this entire time?"

6

MERLOT

Merlot stared at Talbot. His heart had known who she was all along, but his mind couldn't accept it.

He'd mourned her for years. He'd done his best to move on from her death.

And there she stood in the very cottage where they'd fallen madly in love.

That love had never died. He had carried it around like a badge of honor on his chest for the world to see. It had hindered his ability to find love again. To live a full life.

He couldn't blame her for that.

She swiped her hands across her face. "I never wanted to lie to you."

Merlot ran a hand across the top of his head.

"You died. I was at your funeral. And now you're here, pretending to be someone else and fucking with my head."

"That is not what I'm doing." She inched closer.

He moved further away, hitting his back against the far wall. His mind went back to the morning his father woke him and told him about the fire and how Daisy and her mother had died. It had destroyed him emotionally and mentally. He'd been a broken man for years. In some ways he still was. "Are you kidding me? I told you about someone I lost. You knew who I was talking about, yet you continued with the charade."

"Charade? This is my life." She pounded her chest. "I died because my mom had to get away from my father. Leaving him wasn't the answer. She tried that and what did it get her? Or me for that matter. We were trapped. The only solution she saw was planning our deaths, but I had no choice. Whether I wanted to or not, I had to go along with it. But let's imagine for one second what would have happened to me if I had stayed."

Merlot couldn't argue with her logic when it came to the past. Her father was a wicked man who had done horrible things.

And not just to her and her mother.

When he worked for the city council, he'd robbed the town, and Merlot's dad tried to run Richard out of Candlewood Falls. His dad continued to fight Richard long after Daisy had died. His father couldn't stand the level of corruption and would always fight.

But each time he lost and Richard came out on top.

It had defeated his father in ways Merlot had never seen.

"If you did not intend to tell me the truth of your identity, why come back here?" Merlot needed a fucking drink, and not a glass of sweet wine either. He needed something stiff and strong. He went to the liquor cabinet and pulled out a bottle of tequila. He took out a short glass, filled it with ice, and poured it to the rim. "Please make me understand."

"As long as my father is alive, I can't ever be the person I used to be." Talbot had the nerve to kick off her heels and make herself comfortable on his sofa. She tucked her feet under her butt, smoothing her dress over her long, toned legs.

Damn fucking legs.

He chugged.

"Claudia has no idea about my past or my connection to this town. I couldn't leave her high and dry. She's been the only constant in my life since my mother died. I owe her."

He leaned against the counter. "I can understand the new identity. I can get past you dying. But I can't stand here and believe you'd come back and not tell me of all people."

"This isn't going to make any of this better, but I'm so relieved you know."

"Nope." He shook his head. "Kind of makes it worse." He sipped his beverage. "How much of what you told me about your current life is a lie?"

"Nothing," she said.

"So, there's a man you're in love with." The word *love* stuck to the roof of his mouth like something bitter. He had no right to be angry over her having someone. He had no claim to her whatsoever. Technically, she was dead and he had done his best to move on.

"Not in the way I presented it. Or in how you're thinking."

"That makes no sense, Daisy."

"My name is Talbot, and that's what you need to call me," she said with a level of conviction he hadn't heard from her since she'd come back to Candlewood Falls.

He had to admit, he enjoyed the fire that illuminated in her gaze. "Okay. But I need you to explain that statement, Talbot."

"I'm going to need one of those in order to do that."

He laughed. "You tried tequila once. It made you throw up."

"A few things have changed in twenty-one years."

He snagged another glass. After preparing her drink, he handed it to her, but he wasn't ready to be so close, so he chose the corner of the bed on the other side of the room. "I'm listening."

She took the tequila and downed the entire liquid.

"You're going to regret that."

"Not as much as I'm going to regret the second one." Gracefully, she rose and strolled to the bar, making herself another drink.

Patiently, he waited until she settled back on the couch.

"You've always been persistent and the only way I could think to get you to back off was to tell you there was someone else because I knew I wouldn't be able to resist you."

"I don't know if I'm supposed to take that as a compliment or not."

She tossed her head back and took her drink like

a shot. Back in high school, they stole liquor from his older brother and did shots. He had to hold her hair back for half an hour that night while it all came back up.

He had a feeling he might be doing that again.

"You didn't have to lie to me about there being a man in your life if you didn't want me," he said.

"You don't get it." She laughed. "It wasn't exactly a lie. I am in love with someone."

He arched a brow. That wasn't the answer he wanted to hear, but he did want the truth. "Who?"

"For a smart man, sometimes you're a dumbass." She let out a long breath. "When I was yanked out of bed in the middle of the night by my mom and tossed on a bus bound for God knows where, I cried for hours because I had to leave you and I didn't even get a chance to say goodbye, but I was more worried about you."

"Why?"

"Because I knew the plan. I knew they were going to tell you I was dead. If that had been me, I would have been heartbroken. At least I knew you were alive and had a chance at a good life. A happy one. But the thing I never anticipated was I never got closure."

"What does this have to do with who you love?" he asked.

"Oh my God." She jumped to her feet, stumbling in his direction, reaching for his drink.

"Nope. You've had enough." He jerked his hand away.

She fell backward on the bed, stretched her arms wide, and sighed. "Jesus, Merlot. You're the man. You're who I love. I can't believe I had to spell it out for you like that."

"You're drunk."

She scooted closer to the headboard. "The first time you told me you loved me, you were stoned." She hugged one of the pillows. "Do you have any weed? It's legal now."

He burst out laughing. "Even if I did, you are not getting high while you're already this wasted."

"You're no fun."

He took another long, slow sip. He let the liquor ease down his throat while he contemplated her words.

Neither one of them were the same teenagers who made love in this very bed. They were both in love with a memory. He'd held on to Daisy because deep down he knew she and her mother had an exit strategy, but he never wanted to believe they would ever execute it.

There had been a part of him that needed to accept they were gone.

"How could you have dated Rachel?" she asked.

He jerked his head. "You know about that? When I mentioned dating Malbec's ex, I didn't mention a name."

"The scandal about what happened to her a couple of years ago made national news." She hiccupped.

Not a good sign.

"That was one of the biggest mistakes of my life," Merlot admitted. "But it was a very short-lived relationship." He pushed himself back and pulled her close. He wanted to feel her in his arms. It wasn't a need to know the past, but to get a sense of the present.

The truth had come out and he didn't have a grip on his emotions.

All he knew was that he needed to know what might be and the only way to do that was to start over.

But could they do that with a secret they both had to keep?

She snuggled into his body, wrapping her arm

around his stomach. "Don't you have a response to what I said?" She hiccupped again.

It was only a matter of time before she made a beeline to the bathroom. Looked like he was going to have a houseguest for the night.

"I honestly have so many emotions, and they are clashing around in my brain like wildfire." He lifted her chin with his thumb and forefinger. "The girl I love died and I get she has to stay dead. We can't go back and make up for lost time. Like you said, you're Talbot Grant. You're an entirely different person."

"In name, yes. But I am still me." She covered her mouth and belched.

He sat up, leaned across the bed, and found a garbage can. She might not make it to the bathroom, and he didn't really want to spend his night cleaning up vomit. "I think it's best if we table this conversation for when you're sober."

She shoved the trash can out of the way. "No. I want to do this now."

"All right, but you won't like what I have to say." He stood, needing a little distance. He couldn't get it all out while he held her in his arms. "You can't be in Candlewood Falls. As much as I would love to see what you and I could be together in this new life you created for yourself, how our two worlds could line up, it can't ever be. Not now. Not ever. Your father is going to come here and announce his run for governor. He's a cruel and vindictive man. He won't just go after you. He'll come after me and my family. I can't allow that. The best thing you can do is leave as soon as possible. If you must stay while your boss is here, hide in your house. We shouldn't be seen together because I won't be the only one who figures it out. This is a small town and people don't forget. We have a memorial for you and your mom in the park."

"I know. I saw it."

He closed his eyes and took in a deep breath. "You're the one who doesn't get it now." He blinked. "Your dad didn't want that memorial. He fought my parents on it. He didn't believe you were dead. He approached me at your funeral and wondered why I didn't pretend to die with you."

She gasped, but it became like a gurgle mixed with a burp. "That's terrible." Her words slurred.

"It didn't end there. He still owns the land your home was on."

"I saw a new house there."

Merlot nodded. "He rents it out. But he makes his presence known here in Candlewood Falls, and every once in while he shows up with his conspiracy theories. If he were to see me with a woman who resembles his daughter, he'd dig and it—"

She bolted from the bed, shoving him aside, and raced across the room. She knocked over the lamp on the end table in the process.

The door to the bathroom slammed shut.

He sighed. Thankfully, the light didn't break. He picked it up and slowly made his way across the small cottage. He shouldn't have been so blunt. It had physically hurt him to say the words, but it had to be done.

There was no way he could be with Talbot.

It didn't matter that there was love in his heart. Everything he felt belonged to someone who needed to stay buried. Not just for her sake, but for his. It was a selfish move on his part, but if he didn't do it, he'd end up even more broken.

He heard the sound of the toilet flushing and then the water running.

She stepped from the bathroom. Her face was as white as a ghost. "I used your toothbrush."

"Good to know." He pursed his lips.

"Don't give me that look. We've been intimate. What difference does it make?"

"Come on." He guided her to the bed. "I've got some clothes you can sleep in."

"I should go home."

"You're not going anywhere tonight." He helped her out of her dress and put her in a pair of shorts and a T-shirt, ignoring the overwhelming pull to climb into his bed and hold her all night.

Fuck it.

She needed a little comfort in her life. It was the least he could do.

He climbed in next to her and wrapped his arms around her body.

"I'm sorry," she whispered between sobs. "I never meant to hurt you."

"The truth is, you didn't. Life did." He pressed his lips against her forehead. "Get some sleep." It was going to be one hell of a long night.

7

CARTER

arter sat at the kitchen table, staring at the computer screen. He'd questioned many things in his past, but none weighed heavier on his heart than the night he sent Talbot away. Tentatively, he reached out and touched the screen. Tears burned his dry eyes.

"What are you looking at?" Weezer strolled into the kitchen. She snagged a mug and poured some coffee before refilling his cup.

He turned the computer. "This is our grandson, Corbin."

"Oh, my. He looks a lot like Merlot. Although, I can see some of Talbot in him."

"He has the shape of her face, but those eyes and

that smile is all our son." Carter sighed. "He's going to be twenty-one in a week."

"That's hard to believe." Weezer traced the image with her forefinger. "That's our first grandchild."

"And he doesn't even know we exist." Carter leaned back. He didn't resent Talbot. Not one bit. She did exactly what she'd been told to do. What she needed to do to survive. He was proud of her for what she'd done with her life. From all accounts, she'd raised a fine young man. He couldn't fault Talbot for anything.

But he could blame himself for one more secret this family had to bear.

"I wish we could meet him." Weezer squeezed his thigh.

No one in this town, except maybe Silas, understood their relationship.

He'd fallen in love with Weezer when he'd been a teenager himself. People thought he'd been crazy. Weezer already had a reputation for being eccentric. She'd done that to keep the world at arm's length. Her family could be intense, especially her grandfather, all because of secrets. "You know that's not possible."

"Like you haven't thought about it," Weezer said.

"Of course I have, but it's too dangerous for him and Talbot."

"You got out of bed at three in the morning." She tapped his leg. "You've been sitting in front of this computer ever since, and don't try to tell me you haven't. I know you, Carter River. I can guarantee that you've been doing one of two things. Or both."

He chuckled. "Oh, yeah. And what do you think I've been working on?"

"Either a way to take down Richard Berkin—that fucking asshole. Or a way for us to meet our first-born grandchild."

The love of his life knew him well.

"My contact in DC said there is an ongoing hush-hush investigation into Richard."

"About what?"

"Campaign funds for one," Carter said. "But also his second wife and abuse allegations."

"Shocker." Weezer pulled the computer closer. "I don't think I've told you enough how proud I am of you for getting rid of the corruption in our local sheriff's office."

"I love you for that, but it was a little too late for Talbot and her mom."

"You did everything you could for them."

Carter wanted to believe that, but he still felt as though he failed them and his son.

And now his grandson.

"There's more," he said. "My contact told me a woman has come forward with allegations of sexual misconduct. It hasn't come out yet because he believes there are more women and he wants to build a stronger case."

"You're getting involved, aren't you?" Weezer continued to gaze at the screen, mesmerized by the image that stared back.

"Damn right, I am. A day hasn't gone by where I haven't thought about all the things that man got away with. I have an entire filing cabinet filled with information I've gathered on him and I've already called my assistant to start scanning. I'm going to send it. I have no idea if it will help, but it will give them more to go on."

"You're a good man." Weezer tilted her head. "What about this boy? What are we going to do about him? He's our family."

"I don't know yet. He's currently deployed, but I've learned he's coming Stateside early."

"I wonder if Talbot knows that."

Carter shrugged. "Considering how much he

looks like Merlot, it wouldn't be good for Corbin to come to Candlewood Falls."

"I can't believe she named him Corbin. That was a dangerous move. She had to have known that's a family name. Did you say anything to her about it?"

"No. It was my mother's maiden name. Not many people know that. Hell, most people forget I changed my name to River when we got married so our children could have the same name as the winery."

"Your mother was an ornery woman who didn't like me much. She didn't even come to our wedding. She barely acknowledged our children."

"But she did have a thing for Merlot," Carter said. "She sent him, and only him, a birthday card every year until she died when he was twelve."

"That always burned my ass." Weezer pushed the computer aside. "I know I made a million and one mistakes as a parent. I hurt my kids and I'm sometimes ashamed for what I did. But at least I can say everything was in the name of protecting them. Your mom only wanted to hurt us."

"I won't argue that point, but Merlot never did understand and he took her gestures as a sign of love. Not as a dig at us." Carter had resented his mother for years for her unwillingness to accept

Weezer. When Riesling had run off with Theo, he worried he'd been doing the exact same thing. Only, Weezer wasn't an abusive human being. She was a kind and loving woman. Her only crime was keeping her family's secret and being wildly misunderstood.

Theo was a criminal.

"I should have never continued to try to reconcile with my mother," Carter said. "But Corbin's name doesn't concern me. My mother has been dead for years and no one in this town utters her name. She's not even a blip on the radar. It's who Corbin looks like that worries me, so I hesitate to bring him here."

"You've seriously considered it? I was just daydreaming." Weezer's eyes went wide.

"Talbot never went home last night." The moment Carter watched his son chase Talbot out into the vineyard, he knew all bets were off. Talbot was beyond frazzled. There was no way she'd be able to hold it together. Keeping her true identity from the man she loved was eating her alive and Carter couldn't expect her to keep doing it. He could only hope that Merlot would forgive him.

"Shit," Weezer mumbled. "Do you think he knows?"

"I'd bet my life on it."

"I don't know if I'm relieved or petrified." Weezer

stood and eased into Carter's lap, wrapping her arms around his shoulders. "All of our children have suffered in one way or another from our decisions. But that is one thing I honestly believed would never come back and haunt us."

"But it has and now it looks like we get to deal with it head-on because Merlot is walking up the porch steps."

Merlot

Merlot figured Talbot would be passed out for hours, especially after the night she'd had. She'd been sick multiple times and he truly felt bad for the hangover she would experience. However, his own brain suffered with the billion unanswered questions that swirled around like a twister.

He banged on his parents' door. It was only six in the morning, but the light was on and his parents had always been early risers.

His mother greeted him with a smile and mug of steaming coffee. "Good morning, son," she said. "What brings you by so early?"

"Where's Dad?"

"In the kitchen," his father called.

He kissed his mother's cheek, took the cup, and strolled through his childhood home. He plopped himself at the table and rubbed a hand over his unshaven face. "I need to talk and I don't know where else to turn."

"What's wrong?" his father asked. "You look like shit."

"I feel worse." He had no idea where to begin. Or even if his parents would believe him, but if he could trust anyone, it would be his folks. They might be an odd couple and they occasionally did questionable things, but no matter what, he could always say they had been there for him, even when he didn't believe they were.

When Daisy died, they had held him when he cried like a baby and thought his world had come crashing down. They had encouraged him to grieve in whatever capacity that felt right. They never judged or belittled the love he and Daisy—Talbot—had shared.

They were right by his side when the shit hit the fan with Rachel.

Every moment in life, his parents had been his rock. They hadn't liked it when he walked away from the family business, and they had voiced it loud and clear, but they were also proud of the man he'd become.

"There is no easy way to say this, and it's going to blow your mind." He glanced between his parents, who stared him with an unnerving gaze. Taking in a deep breath, he let it out slowly. He still couldn't believe it himself. Whenever he thought he was okay with the idea that the love of his life was still alive, he remembered the day he stood at her gravesite. It had been the single worst day of his life. "Talbot isn't who she says she is."

"Who is she?" his father asked with a deadpan expression.

His mother took his hand and squeezed.

He blinked. The gravity of the situation hit his gut like a bullet tearing through his body. "Jesus Christ, you know."

"Know what?" His father lifted his mug and sipped as if this were any other morning conversation around the breakfast table.

"Oh my fucking God." He pushed his chair back, knocking it over, and stood. "I can't fucking believe it. How long have you known she was alive?"

"Who exactly are we talking about?" his father asked.

"I'm not in the mood for games. I've had one hell of a fucking night. So just be honest with me. When did you figure out Talbot was Daisy?"

"Sit down, son," his mother said, resting his hand on his shoulder.

"I'd rather stand." He shrugged it off.

"What did she tell you?" his father asked.

"Jesus. That's obvious."

"No. It's not." His father leaned back in his chair and folded his massive arms across his chest. "You came here to talk and I appreciate that, but I'm not sure Talbot told you the whole story."

Merlot's mouth popped open. "What more could there be? Her mother faked their deaths in order to protect them."

His dad glanced toward his mom and if he thought his world had imploded when he'd been seventeen, he'd been mistaken.

This moment was a hundred times worse.

"What the hell did you do, Dad?"

"What I thought was best at the time for everyone," his father said with a stern tone. "It was a last resort. I tried like hell to get that man arrested. The first time poor Talbot ended up with a broken nose." His father pounded his chest. "I had to live with that. It still pains me what that man did to his family. I never wanted to send them away. I tried to find other solutions for months, but when he shot at Talbot's mother, I saw the writing on the wall. They would have ended up really dead if I hadn't done what I did."

"Your father's right," his mom said softly. "You don't know what he went through after they left. The tears. The agony of watching you suffer. That was the last thing we wanted to do."

Merlot raked a hand through his hair. Part of him could forgive his parents for sending Talbot and her mother far away from that bastard. But the moment she came back, they should have told him. They should have encouraged her to tell him. They of all people knew what her death had done.

"All those things that went wrong at the event last night." He pointed to his mother. "You did that, didn't you?"

She nodded.

"You never wanted me to find out. You wanted to keep me in the dark and away from Talbot and you had her playing along."

"She knew it was what was best. The pull the two of you have for each other is still so very strong and with her father—"

"Oh, fuck that," Merlot interrupted his dad. "You did it to protect your own ass."

His dad slammed his hands on the table and stood. "Don't you dare come into my home and talk to me that way. I'm still your father, no matter how old you get, and I demand respect. It kills me and your mom to see you hurting like this. We have had to live with it, but we have always known we did the right thing when it comes to Talbot. I'm sorry that you were collateral damage in that. But we had to get her away from Richard. He was going to kill her if we didn't. Something you seem to have forgotten."

"Oh no. Trust me. I won't ever forget what he did to Talbot." He placed his hand over his heart. "You fail to understand that I'm not angry over you saving her. I can get on board with that. But I can't live with the lies that followed the second she came to town. The way you snuck around to try to keep it from me when you knew damn well I was struggling because I knew in my soul of souls who Talbot was. You should have come to me and all of you should have told me about—fuck it. I'm done with all of you. I quit the winery and I quit this fucking family."

"That's a little harsh," his mom said. "Not to mention rash."

Merlot laughed. "Right before Dad's mom passed, she told me how much she disliked Mom. It bothered me because I knew it was unfounded. I had to live with how misunderstood Mom was all these years and I've always laughed it off. But the one thing that Grandma said that always stuck with me was how manipulative Mom was and you know what? She was right."

"You can stop right now, son," his father said. "I will not allow you to speak to your mother that way, especially when you use my mom as the source. Talk about a manipulative woman. She used her relationship with you to keep me in her life when I should have cut her out long ago. She didn't love me, much less ever respect me." His father held up a hand. "Your mom and I have made some horrible mistakes with you kids, which have cost us. And yes, your mother can be a little underhanded at times. But the difference between your mom and mine, is that your mother loves you with every fiber of her being. Everything she has ever done has been to protect this family. My mother only wanted to see me and Weezer get divorced. Did you know that she threw a party a day after that happened and then sent your mom a dozen dead roses? Talk about a bitch move. That was the day I knew, and I never spoke to her again. But I also never took her away from you. So get off your fucking high horse. Be pissed off all you want at the situation, but don't you dare treat your mom with anything but the love and respect she deserves."

Merlot wasn't going to listen to any of it. He didn't care that most of it made sense. Or that he knew his father was right.

They still lied to him about the one thing that had mattered to him most and so had Talbot. He couldn't reconcile those two things.

"I'm sorry for that comparison." He nodded. "However, that doesn't change what you did or how I feel. Consider this my resignation, and it starts immediately. I need to leave town."

"Take time off, but don't leave." His mother inched closer.

He took a step back, and she thankfully gave him the space.

"I apologize for yelling." His father blew out a puff of air. "Please don't leave. But I agree with your mom. Take all the time you need to sort through things and we're here when you want to talk."

"There's nothing left to say. The lies and secrets that keep turning up in this family have done me in. First Eliza Jane and how we stole this winery from her family. Then Trey and the black market baby ring.

Not to mention everything that went down with Riesling. Now me? What's next?" He waved his hands. "I'm seriously done. You don't need me. I'm a swing in the winery anyway. I'm like the kid you don't know what to do with, so you give him the job no one else wants."

"That's not true," his mom said. "We're trusting you and Zinny with—"

"Mom, save it for someone who cares. I've got a flight to book." He turned and marched toward the door.

His parents called after him, but he didn't bother glancing over his shoulder. He had something else he had to take care of and the closer he got to the cottage, the more his blood boiled.

He stormed into his house with his heart in his throat. His anger filled his soul like a bad rash. He couldn't get past it. Even after calming down a little at his parents', the rage bubbled into every muscle of his body.

She'd lied about one of the most important aspects of her disappearance.

He slammed the door shut. It rattled so hard, it knocked one of the pictures off the wall.

Talbot startled awake, brushing the hair from her face. She groaned. "What the hell?"

"Get the fuck out," he yelled. He sucked in a deep breath. He needed to control his emotions. He hadn't been this full of fury since Rachel.

She stared at him with a pale face.

He had no sympathy left. No empathy. No pain. Only rage in his heart.

"What's going on?" She pulled the covers to her chin.

"Get your things and get the hell out of my house."

"Merlot, what happened? Why are you so angry?" Tears filled her eyes. "I know I got a little out of control last night and it's all kind of fuzzy, but—"

"Stop talking and leave. Don't make me pick you up out of that bed and toss you out, because I will."

Her hands trembled as she tucked her hair behind her ears and crawled to the edge of the mattress. "Not until you tell me what's going on."

He laughed. "You failed to mention to me last night that it was my father who put you on that bus twenty-one years ago and that my mother was standing right next to him when he did it."

"You talked to your parents? You told them you knew I was alive?"

"What the fuck did you think I was going to do? I needed someone to talk to about all this. Stupid me,

I thought I could trust them. How the hell was I supposed to know they were the ones who set the entire fake death up in the first place. They have lied to me my entire life and I'm fucking done." He clenched his fists as he marched to the bar and lifted the tequila, not bothering to pour a glass. He chugged straight from the bottle.

"I think it's a little early for that."

"I really don't give a shit what you think." He pointed to the door. "I'm not going to say it again." He took another gulp, letting the alcohol seep into his brain.

She climbed from the bed and dared to move closer.

He held up his hand.

"We're not done talking. There are things I need to tell you."

"I don't want to know anything about you or your life. Nothing. Nada. Zilch. This last lie just made it damn fucking easy to forget I ever met you."

"I don't believe that," she said softly.

He set the bottle down and gathered up her clothes and handed them to her. "Don't let the door hit you on the way out."

"There's no reason to be this way. Your parents

were doing what my mother asked. They were only trying—"

"Please, do me a favor and leave because I don't want to be the kind of man who takes you by the arm and forcibly tosses you out. But I will." He lowered his chin. "Hand to God, I swear I will turn into something I won't be proud of."

"Merlot, I really need to tell you—"

"Nope. You and I have nothing to say to one another. I will be booking a flight this afternoon and getting the fuck out of this godforsaken shithole of a town. We will never lay eyes on each other again."

Tears rolled down Talbot's cheeks.

A pang of guilt filled his soul.

She'd been seventeen when she'd been taken from him. A child. A victim.

But the woman standing before him was a grown-ass adult. And she'd lied to him about so many things.

He opened the door and she scurried past him, pausing at the opening.

"Please, you have a—"

He slammed it shut. Leaning against the wooden object, he closed his eyes tight. For the first time in his life, he felt truly alone.

8

———

TALBOT

Talbot spent the next twenty-four hours nursing the worst hangover of her life, only to be compounded by the inability to stop crying.

She'd called and texted Merlot a dozen or so times.

He refused to respond.

For all she knew, he was on a plane to Timbuktu.

She pulled the covers to her chin and tried to focus on some stupid reality show her son loved to watch. She could never understand why Corbin liked shows like this, but she always enjoyed watching them with him whenever she could.

God, she missed that boy so much.

She hadn't been thrilled the day he dropped out of college after his first year and told her he had joined the Army. He hadn't even asked her what her thoughts were on his decision. He'd just up and enlisted.

He'd been lost and she wondered if maybe she'd pushed him too hard about his education. Some of his friends were taking a gap year and perhaps she should have let him do the same. However, the Army had turned out to be the best thing that had ever happened to that kid.

He thrived in the environment. He'd gotten his bachelor's degree in record time and was now an officer. He had the start to an incredible career. She couldn't be prouder.

Ding-dong.

The noise halted her tears for the first time since she ran from Merlot's cottage.

She leaped from the sofa, raced to the door, and pulled it open. "Oh, hi, Weezer," she managed. Her disappointment that it wasn't Merlot rang full force from her voice. "I'm sorry, I'm not in the mood for visitors."

"I'm sure you're not, but I'm not just anyone." Weezer held up a basket. "I come with homemade bread, my world-famous macaroni and cheese that you used to gobble up like there was no tomorrow, and some sugar cookies with peanut butter cups in the middle. I remember how much you loved those."

A smile spread across Talbot's face. "That's very kind of you."

"Don't tell anyone. I have a reputation to uphold in this town of being the resident bitch."

Talbot laughed. "Come in." She couldn't think of any good reason to send Weezer packing. The woman had never been anything but generous to Talbot. Many of the other kids growing up were terrified of Weezer, but not Talbot. She knew the real woman behind the mask. She also knew never to get on her bad side. "How's Merlot?"

"I'm not exactly sure except he hasn't left the cottage and I'm pretty sure he's been drunk the entire time. He won't talk to me or Carter. I know the twins have tried, but he threw an empty bottle of tequila at them, so they told me until he sobers up, they won't have anything to do with him. Those three haven't always gotten along."

"I remember."

"Malbec stopped by to see him and Merlot let him in, but the conversation went downhill quickly."

Talbot sat on the sofa and ripped the lid off the pasta. She took the fork Weezer had provided and dug in, realizing she hadn't eaten since the party. She moaned as her taste buds lit up. "I've tried a million times to make this, and it has never tasted this good."

"I'll give you the recipe, but you can never tell anyone my secret ingredients." Weezer made herself comfortable in the chair kitty-corner. "You should know that everyone in our family now knows."

"That wasn't smart and they all must hate me."

Weezer leaned over and patted her leg. "No one in this family could ever have bad feelings for you."

"Merlot certainly does."

"He's hurting. Give him time and he'll come around," Weezer said.

"Why did you have to tell everyone? That's just putting me at greater risk."

Weezer shook her head. "It's an extra layer of protection, especially since your father rolled into town today."

"Fuck," Talbot muttered, dropping her fork in her lap. "That's the last thing Merlot needs."

"You were always putting him before yourself." Weezer sighed. "I came here to warn you, so you could avoid town for two days. Once he's gone, you should be able to move about freely again."

"This is so fucked up. I should have never come here and if I could go back in time and change that decision, I would." Even though she'd mentally lost her appetite, her stomach betrayed her mind and it growled. She continued to pick at the food Weezer brought. "I've been avoiding my boss, and she's wondering what the hell is up with me. And I'm sure Carter told you about Corbin."

"He did." Weezer nodded.

"I want to tell Merlot. He should know, but how would I tell my son that I've lied to him his whole life? That I betrayed a trust so great. He'll never forgive me."

"If he knew all the facts, he absolutely will. Just like Merlot will."

"I tried to tell Merlot about Corbin yesterday, but he threw me out. There was so much venom in his words. I've never seen him so angry and hateful before."

"That wasn't about you, dear. That has to do with a world of lies my family had kept. They keep coming unearthed and this was just one more that Carter and I piled on."

"It doesn't matter. I don't think there is any chance we can come back from this."

"I have faith, and you should too," Weezer said. "But there is something else I need to discuss with you. Carter and I debated if we should or not, but considering how all this got started by either lies, or omitting the truth, we decided on transparency."

"Now you're scaring me."

"This could be considered good news." Weezer scooted forward, holding Talbot's gaze. "Carter has been talking with some lawyer friends of his in DC. One of them works for the Department of Justice. His name is Joseph. He's been compiling a case for the last two years against your father. Carter has a load of paperwork on all the things Richard did here in Candlewood Falls."

"But Carter couldn't prove any of it."

Weezer held up her finger. "That's not entirely true. Your father paid off people and got away with it. But thanks to my brilliant husband for keeping everything and the work Joseph has been doing, they are getting close to having strong enough evidence to indict your father. They have a little more work to do, but imagine a world where you don't have to be afraid anymore. Where you can be here in Candle-wood Falls and not care if anyone knows who you really are and your son can get to know his father and the rest of his family."

A guttural sob filled Talbot's throat. She gasped. "I can't even go there," she managed. "Besides living my life for all these years as Talbot Grant, I'm not sure I ever want people to know the truth. It's one thing for you all to know. Or even my son to meet his father. But I would never want it to make the news. I can see the headline now."

Weezer grabbed her hand. "Carter and I have always wanted to see Richard pay for the things he's done. There is no questioning that. But I will admit that I have selfish reasons for wanting that man out of your life. I want to know my grandson."

"I never intended to keep him from you."

"I know that." Weezer moved to the sofa and wrapped her arm around Talbot. "None of this is your fault. You didn't ask for this to happen. You, your mother, even your son, are all victims. Putting Richard away for good has always been in the back of Carter's mind. He never believed he could bring you and Merlot together again. But now that it's happened, he's more determined than ever."

"You have always been so good to me. I'm sorry that I've—"

"Hush, child. There is no reason for you to apologize. I'll text you once I know your father has left town, and then I want you to go to Merlot and do your best to talk some sense into that man."

"If he threw a bottle at the twins, he'll toss a perfectly good case of wine at me."

Weezer laughed. "I know my son. And if he was serious about leaving town, he would have done it already. He needs a little time to get over his bruised ego, and then he'll be ready. But you've got to figure out how you're going to deal with your own web of lies so they don't come back and bite you in the ass. And remember, Carter and I are here for you, always. We will help you navigate whatever you need."

"No matter what happens, I need to be the one to tell Merlot about his son."

"Carter and I have already discussed that and we agree. We are, however, concerned about the timing. We want to keep you and Corbin safe. All these secrets are killing us."

Outside of her own mother and Claudia, the River family had been the only place Talbot had felt love.

At least one thing hadn't changed.

Merlot

Merlot had finally sobered up and showered. His rage had turned to a mix of loneliness and confusion.

He sat at the kitchen table, staring at a flight to the Bahamas but couldn't pull the trigger.

His mind was a haze of misplaced bitterness.

He owed his parents one whopper of an apology.

Snapping his computer closed, he lifted his cell and stared at the unread messages from Talbot. He hadn't been able to bring himself to read them until now.

Talbot: *We need to talk. Please call me.*

Talbot: *I understand you're mad. I'm not asking for your forgiveness. I'm not expecting anything from you. I need to talk to you. There is something you need to know.*

Talbot: *This is important. I wouldn't keep bothering you if it wasn't.*

Talbot: *There is one more truth that needs to be told and you need to hear it from me.*

He tossed his phone to the table. He couldn't even imagine what that was and he wasn't sure he wanted to find out.

A tap at the door sent his hangover into overdrive.

"Open up, little brother," Chablis' voice rang out. "I've got a key and I'm not afraid to use it."

"The door's unlocked," he yelled.

Chablis strolled into the cottage carrying a ginger ale in one hand. "I'm fucking sicker than a dog with this kid." She tossed her purse on the sofa and made a beeline for the pantry. She found a bag of pretzels and pulled up a chair. "I'm also hungry all the time, which makes no sense, but at least I'm not throwing up."

"I guess that's good news." He folded his arms. "I take it you're here as the next wave to tell me what an asshole I am."

"Pretty much." She smiled before chomping on her snack. "But in all fairness, I'd also be pissed at Mom and Dad. I'd probably behave the same way." She waved another treat in the air. "However, I understand why they did what they did, including trying to keep you from Talbot. I mean, shit. When you said she kissed like Daisy, I guess you meant it."

"We can't call her that," Merlot said. "We have to remember she's Talbot. Her safety is at stake."

"At least I know you still have a heart."

He chuckled. "I only lost my mind for a day."

"You really hurt Dad. He's been sulking like I've never seen him before."

"I will never forget the weeks following the funeral. Dad acted like he'd lost his best friend. I thought it was because I was in so much pain, but now I know it was the beginning of another secret and one he really had no choice but to keep."

"I'm glad you see it that way." Chablis reached across the table and took his hand. "This family is highly dysfunctional. We have a boatload of pain, and I've been on the receiving end of it more than once. When Mom refused to tell Malbec the big bad dark secret and he abandoned me and then everything that happened with Dax, I thought I would die. But the one thing I've learned is that all that brought us back together and we are stronger than ever, even if our mom is still stranger than shit. She's already planning on how she will win that damn race."

"She cheats every year."

Chablis rolled her eyes. "I can't believe I'm going to say this, but thank God, I'm pregnant and can say, sorry Mom, I'm not going to be in that race with you."

"I fake twisted my ankle last year, so I'll have to devise a better excuse. Zinny is out. So are the twins. We need them running the wine booth."

"Sounds like you're taking back that resignation that Mom is so terrified you might actually follow through on." Chablis smiled.

"I don't know, maybe." He shrugged. He had no desire to go back to being a parole officer. Those days were over, although he did miss carrying a gun on a regular basis. "But I'm still taking a few more days off to clear my head. I'm not sure I can be around our folks without saying something I will regret."

"What about Talbot?"

"I have no idea what to do about her." Merlot still couldn't wrap his brain around his rage or where it originated. He'd been incredibly and unreasonably cruel. However, he wasn't sure there was a place for her in his life. "I need to apologize to her as well."

"I'm glad you're being a decent human being."

"The only problem is I'm not prepared to face her just yet." Merlot knew he needed to get his head out of his ass and put on his big boy pants. But that didn't mean he and Talbot would mean anything to each other. There was too much history, too much pain, and there was no going back. "Is it a douche move to text her an *I'm sorry*."

"Oh my God. Yes. At least call her."

"I can't. Not yet."

"And why not?" Chablis asked. "What are you afraid of?"

"That I'll either fly off the handle and be an even bigger prick, or worse. Take her to bed."

Chablis laughed. "At least you're being honest."

"Unlike the rest of our family."

"Stop it. I don't believe there are any more skeletons in that closet."

He arched a brow. "That means there could be more in other closets."

"We'll leave those for the twins."

"Christ. Those two? They've had it easier than Zinny."

"That is true," Chablis said. "But seriously, let your emotions settle, and then go talk to Talbot. You owe her an in-person apology. You need to at least give her that."

"You're right."

Knock, knock.

"What is this? Grand fucking Central Station?" he muttered. "It's open."

His father stepped inside. "Hey."

Merlot stood and quickly closed the gap, feeling like a kid. He wrapped his arms around his dad. "I'm sorry. You didn't deserve the things I said."

"I'm sorry too." His father gave him a big bear hug. "It's all water under the bridge, son, and I would have been pretty angry at me too." He took a step back.

"I'm going to head back to work." Chablis waved and scurried out the door.

"Now that we've got that out of the way," his father said. "I've got some troubling news."

"What's that?"

"Richard Berkin is in town," his dad said. "Your mother went to Talbot's to let her know of the situation so she can lay low. I'm going to suggest that you do the same. I don't know if you've spoken to Talbot, but if you do, I think it's best that the two of you are not seen anywhere together."

"I haven't talked to her yet." Merlot sighed. "How long is that asshole here for?"

"A couple of days?"

"I'll wait until he's gone and she and I have both had a chance to cool off before I reach out to her."

His father arched a brow. "While I don't want you to risk going anywhere near her right now, are you sure it's wise to let all this fester? I know this is all a lot to take, but I don't want to see it go unresolved."

"I'll text her and tell her we can talk when he leaves town."

His dad nodded. "I want you to know I feel terrible about what happened yesterday."

"So do I, Dad. I'll call Mom and make sure I make things right with her."

"We love you and all we ever wanted was to—"

"I know. We don't have to keep rehashing this." He squeezed his father's biceps. "I promise I won't lose my shit again."

9

MERLOT

Merlot had successfully avoided Talbot's phone calls for three days. Besides wanting to make sure her father was back in DC, he needed to ensure all his emotions and thoughts were in check. He'd had two long talks with his sister Zinny, who, for someone so young, was insightful as shit.

The bottom line was he was still in love with Talbot. It didn't matter that she'd changed her name and had a new life. Deep down, she was still the same person who had left him twenty-one years ago. His struggle to get past the lies had more to do with how much it hurt that he'd been the only one in the dark.

He'd suffered insurmountable grief and his

parents had watched. If felt like a betrayal wrapped in a layer of protection.

Talk about a contradiction.

Only, he'd been grieving the wrong thing.

He'd lost the love of his life. He could accept that, but she'd had a good life. A happy one. And that he could wrap his brain around.

"I'm sorry that it took three days for this." Merlot stepped through the door. "I'm sorry—"

"We need to talk." She glanced at her watch. "I have maybe ten minutes to get this out, so do me a favor and shut up and listen."

"You don't get to bark orders at me." He stuffed his hands in his pockets and followed her to the kitchen. "I'm trying to say I'm sorry for how I behaved. You didn't deserve that and I was wrong."

"Apology accepted. All is forgiven."

He arched a brow. "Just like that."

"Yup." She nodded as if she were a bobblehead. "Would you like a beer or something?" she asked as she paced in front of the fridge. Her nervous energy filled the room like a thick cloud of smoke.

"Do I need one?"

"I don't know. You might. And I'm going to have one." She ducked her head into the refrigerator and pulled out two, pushing one across the counter. "I sent you a text after you tossed me out on my ass—"

"I said I was sorry."

"Yeah. I know and it's fine. Please, let me get through this before another secret is unraveled the wrong way."

He laughed. "Because there's a right way to—"

"I have a son," she blurted out. "No. We have a son. His name is Corbin. He's going to be twenty-one in a few days." She lifted her beer and clanked it against his. "Cheers."

He stood in the kitchen with his mouth hanging open.

"Oh. And there are two more things."

"You've got to be joking. I haven't even digested that piece of news." Him? A father. And he missed it? Fuck. His mind swirled. His pulse raged so fast he thought he might have a heart attack.

The only good news was he didn't want to wring her pretty little neck.

"You named him Corbin?" He blinked.

"Yeah. But we'll have to talk about that later because he'll be here in a few minutes."

"Jesus, I need to sit down." He gripped the counter. "How did that happen?"

"I'll get into that later. The second thing is he

thinks—"

Corbin burst through the door. "Mom. Where are you?"

Merlot swallowed. His son. His adult son. He wrangled in his anger. There was no place for that now. What was done was done. He couldn't change the past and Talbot wasn't to blame. She'd done the best she could with what she'd been given.

A young man wearing Army fatigues stepped into the kitchen. He dropped his rucksack by the hallway and blinked.

"Corbin. It's so good to see you." Talbot raced to her son, wrapping her arms around his shoulders.

Merlot stood there like a lump on a log. It was like looking into a mirror of his youth.

Corbin must have noticed the resemblance because he lifted his mother off the ground and set her to the side, glaring. "Who the hell are you?"

"I need you to stay calm," Talbot said. "This is going to be a bit of a shock."

"What's going on, Mom?"

"This is Merlot River. He's your father." Talbot smiled weakly.

Corbin lowered his chin and narrowed his stare.

Merlot knew that look well. He'd seen his father use it often when he'd been pissed. It was also an expression Merlot used right before he used his fist to punch out a boy who'd made disparaging remarks about Talbot. He braced himself for impact.

"You fucking bastard," Corbin said with venom laced to every syllable.

"I won't have you speak like that to your dad." Talbot rested a hand on Corbin's shoulder.

Corbin shifted his gaze. "Are you kidding me? That man didn't even want me. He left you pregnant at seventeen and went off and did whatever the fuck he wanted without a single care in the world."

"That's what you told him about me?" Merlot knew Talbot hadn't gotten a chance to finish everything she'd wanted to tell him before their son came barging in, but damn—that one hurt.

"Are you going to stand there and say it's not true? Are you going to call my mother a liar after everything she's been through?"

"Oh, son. You don't know the half of it," Merlot muttered.

"Don't you ever call me son." Corbin lunged.

Talbot stepped in front of him. "Stop it right now." She pressed her hand on Corbin's chest. "Merlot is right. You don't know the whole story and you're going to sit your ass down in that chair and listen, you hear me, young man?"

"I'm not a child," Corbin said.

"No, you're not. But I'm still your mother and I won't hesitate to grab you by the ear and make you howl." She lifted her hand.

Corbin rubbed his ear.

"Now sit." She pointed to a chair.

This was a side of Talbot he'd never seen before, and damn, he liked it.

"Fine, but don't expect me to believe anything that man has to say. If you want to drink the Kool-Aid, that's your problem." He pulled back a chair, turned it around, and straddled it.

She smacked him, though not hard, on the back side of his head.

"Jesus, Mom. Seriously?" He rubbed his neck. "Is he why you and Mama C came to this town?"

"Mama C?" Merlot took his beer and chugged. "Is that supposed to be Claudia?"

"Yeah. Doesn't he know her?" Corbin folded his arms across the back of the chair. Merlot used to do this when he'd been about Corbin's age. It drove his mother batshit crazy.

Which was why he did it.

"I know who she is, but I literally just found out about you two minutes before you came walking through that door." Perhaps he shouldn't have said that, but this was new territory for all of them.

Corbin jerked his head. "He's bullshitting me, right, Mom? That can't be true. Please tell me he's the one who's lying."

A tear rolled down Talbot's cheek. "All the lies stop right here. Right now."

"Jesus, Mom. So, that's why you'd never tell me anything about my father. What the hell is wrong with him that you didn't want me to know?"

"Absolutely nothing." She turned her gaze and smiled at Merlot. "He's one of the kindest, sweetest men I've ever known. I was madly in love with him when I left this town. But circumstances made it so I could never come back and Merlot could never know about you. I didn't even know I was pregnant when I left."

"I need a fucking drink." Corbin ran a hand across the top of his freshly buzzed head.

"You're not twenty-one yet," Talbot said.

"He fights for this country and his entire world just blew up. And didn't you tell me he will be twenty-one soon? I think the man deserves a beer." Merlot strolled around to the other side of the island and pulled out a cold one. He cracked it open and set it in front of his son.

As weird as that was, it didn't feel strange.

"Thanks, but don't think that wins you any brownie points with me." Corbin took a long, slow sip.

"Not looking for any." Merlot sat and tried not to stare, but it was impossible.

"What?" Corbin pursed his lips.

"Sorry. It's just like looking at myself when I was your age."

"Yeah. Hard not to see the resemblance." Corbin sighed.

Talbot eased into the seat across from Merlot. "You're taking this much better than I thought you would."

"I've wanted to know who my dad was for as long as I can remember. I used to threaten to run away from home if you didn't tell me."

Talbot laughed. "I watched you pack your little suitcase when you were nine. You went to the hotel lobby and tried to check yourself into your own room."

Corbin frowned. "You let me spend the night there and when I came back the next day, you told me a lie."

"There are a lot of things that we need to tell you, but understand your mother did what she had to in order to protect herself and you from a very bad man," Merlot said.

Corbin tilted his head. "I always thought that person was you."

"Trust me. If I or anyone in my family had known of your existence, we wouldn't be sitting in this room right now." Merlot understood the pain that radiated from his son's eyes. It tore through his soul like a rocket. "This is going to be hard, but no can know I'm your father. At least not right now."

"Why the hell not?" Corbin glared. "What about Mama C?"

"She can't know. She doesn't have a clue about my past and I wouldn't want to put her at risk," Talbot said.

"I don't understand, Mom. You need to tell me more before I lose my shit."

Jesus. How could a kid Merlot didn't raise have so many mannerisms and speech patterns that matched his?

"Because my father—the man I ran from all those years ago—would probably kill us all if he ever found out." Talbot rested her hand over Corbin's. "There is one glowing light in all this."

"I'm not sure I see it." Corbin fiddled with his beer can.

"Merlot's parents are wonderful people. They are the ones who set up my death—"

"Excuse me? That makes no fucking sense." Corbin shoved his beverage aside.

"They had to make it so my father thought I was dead," Talbot said.

"I believed that too. I spent the last twenty-one years thinking the love of my life was gone." Did he just say that out loud. Yep. He did.

"Love of your life?" Corbin scoffed.

"I never forgot about your mother, nor did I ever stop loving her. When she showed up here, it was like I took a trip into my childhood. It didn't take long for me to figure it out," Merlot said.

"Which is why we need to be completely transparent with you now and arm you with the knowledge that can protect you from anything bad happening because lying to you and keeping secrets will only hurt you. We've learned that the hard way."

"Ya think?" Corbin shook his head.

Talbot took his hands. "My father's name is Richard Berkin."

"Am I supposed to know who that is?" Corbin asked.

"He's a senator and he's going to make a run for governor of New Jersey," Merlot added.

"So, he's a crooked politician. How does that make him worse than anyone else?" Corbin lifted Talbot's hand and kissed it.

Oh shit. This could go really well. Or really bad. And if Merlot had to put money on this young man's reaction, he'd wager on the latter.

"My father was an incredibly abusive man and—"

"He hit you?" Corbin stood. The same rage that had filled Merlot's body the first time he'd learned of the atrocity filled the air. Corbin turned his attention to Merlot. "And you let it happen."

"We were kids," Talbot said. "And trust me, Merlot and his family tried numerous things, like helping my mom file for divorce."

"But that only made things worse," Merlot admitted. "Richard had half this town in his back pocket. My dad—your grandfather—has been trying to nail that bastard to the wall for years. We believe we might have all the ammunition we finally need, but the system is slow and we need to do it right if we're going to make it stick. That's why—for now—the only people who know about this is our immediate family."

"What does that mean?" Corbin asked. "Who's family? Because all I got is my mom. And I guess you. That is if I decide to accept you."

That was fair. "Besides my parents, I have six siblings and seven nieces and nephews with two more on the way. And if my calculations are correct, a third will be on the way soon."

"Oh really? Who?" Talbot asked.

"Riesling. She's been acting all pissy and it's not because I was a beast for the last few days either," Merlot said.

"Riesling? Merlot? What the hell kinds of names are these? Is everyone named after a wine?" Corbin leaned against the island.

"Me and all my brothers and sisters are. And then Malbec went and kept on with the tradition, but no one else." Merlot had immediately liked Corbin when he waltzed into the kitchen, but he hadn't expected to fall so deeply in love with a perfect stranger.

"I'm glad my mom had better sense," Corbin muttered.

"You might not think that if you knew the story behind your name." Merlot caught Talbot's gaze and arched a brow. "Although, I'm not sure she understood all the nuances of it when I jokingly mentioned wanting to name a kid Corbin when we were seventeen."

"I need to get some fucking air." Corbin took two

steps.

Talbot was on her feet. "Please don't leave. Or at least don't go into town."

"Jesus, Mom. Relax. I'm going to sit outside and take a breath." He kissed her cheek. "I heard what you said about this Richard guy. I understand the secrecy. I won't do anything to put you or anyone else in danger. I saw enough of that in Syria."

Merlot watched as his son meandered out the front door.

"Well, that went better than expected." Talbot turned. "With both of you."

"I'm still in shock."

She held up her fingers, making an inch sign. "There's one teeny-tiny thing that I need to get out in the open so we don't have anything left to fight about."

He dropped his head to the table and groaned. "Lay it on me."

"Your parents have known about Corbin for at least a week."

"Fuck me," he muttered.

"But they had no idea I was pregnant when I left. Hell, I didn't know."

Merlot was done hanging on to the past. He was over all the pain and the anger. It served no purpose.

He had no idea if becoming a father to a grown man had instantly changed him or if he was just tired of it all.

Or both.

It didn't matter.

What did matter was that he had a family to protect and by damn, he wasn't going to lose them twice.

He stood and sauntered across the kitchen. He took Talbot into his arms. "You're a fantastic mother and you did an amazing job with our son."

She buried her face in his chest and sobbed.

"Shit. I didn't mean to make you cry." He kissed her forehead. "Talbot, I mean it. Those aren't empty words."

"I know." She glanced up. "It just means everything to hear you say them."

"Don't slap me."

"Why would I do that?'

"Because I'm going to kiss the hell out of you." He took her mouth in a hot, wild kiss that shouldn't have occurred in the kitchen, but he didn't care. For the first time in a long while, his life made sense. He didn't know what the future held, or if they even had one.

But they had this moment and he'd cherish it for

the rest of his life.

"Oh my God. It's one thing to know I have a father. It's another thing to witness that in the same day," Corbin mumbled. "Is there a room for me, or am I couching it? And is this guy going to be staying over all the time?"

"There's a bedroom all set up for you down the hall," Talbot said with rosy cheeks. "And your father and I haven't gotten that far yet."

"Jesus, Mom. Too much information. Way too much." Corbin snagged his bag. "Not to be an ingrate or anything, but I'm starving. What are we all doing for dinner?"

"Well, since I'd like to get to know you better, but being seen out isn't necessarily smart, we could order a pizza," Merlot said.

"Why can't the two of you date? Like she's not from your past and I'm just the duchy kid who randomly showed up." Corbin arched a brow.

For effect, Merlot gave him the same look.

"Yeah. I get your point." Corbin nodded. "Pizza it is."

"He's a funny kid," Merlot said.

"He takes after me." Talbot smiled.

"I don't know about that. I see a lot of River in that man."

10

TALBOT

Talbot handed the salad bowl to Corbin. "Are you ready for this?" She glanced up at the big house on The River Winery. This had always been her happy place. Her safe harbor. And now she got to share it with her son. Something she thought would never happen.

"Absolutely not." Corbin squared his shoulders. "I always wished for a big family, but I never honestly believed I'd get one, especially like this."

"The Rivers are good people."

"So you keep telling me." Corbin sighed. "I'm sorry for what happened to you as a kid."

"You've got to stop apologizing for something that isn't your fault."

"How come Merlot didn't spend the night yesterday?" Corbin stopped short of the porch. "It's painfully obvious the two of you have so many unresolved feelings for each other and don't tell me it's complicated."

"But it is," she said. "And in all honesty, we can't be together unless my father is put away. It wouldn't be safe for any of us."

"I hear you, and I get what he did was horrible, but you're not a kid anymore. Neither is Merlot."

"I don't want to keep having this argument with you."

"I went to sniper school. And it's not like Merlot isn't good with a weapon."

"Oh my God. Stop. I've told you before, he won't come at us like that. I saw the way he destroyed people. We won't know what hit us. Let Carter work his magic."

"Mom, I only want to see you happy." Corbin smiled. "And Merlot is growing on me."

"Enough to call him Dad?"

"Not there, yet." Corbin laughed. "But at least I know I will be good-looking when I get old."

"Wait until you see his father."

"Ew, Mom. Why do you always have to make things weird?"

She gave her son a nudge toward the steps. "Let's

go meet your grandparents, aunts, uncles, and cousins."

"Now I have heartburn."

Weezer opened the door. She clasped her hands together and rubbed them. "Oh my goodness," she exclaimed. "You must be Corbin. Come here and let me get a good look at you."

He leaned closer to Talbot. "Is she going to squeeze my cheeks?"

"She might, but get her talking and you'll hear all sorts of good stories about your dad."

"That could be fun," Corbin said. "Hi. I take it you're my grandma."

"You can call me that here, but I'm Weezer when we do the three-legged race. That's what everyone in town calls me." Weezer took the salad bowl from his hands and shoved it right back into Talbot's. "My Lord, you look exactly like Merlot." She grabbed his cheeks and tugged.

"Um, Weezer. He's not going to the picnic."

"Oh, yes, he is." Weezer looped her hand around Corbin's waist and pushed him right through the door. "We'll put a baseball cap on his head and keep him in sunglasses. No one will be the wiser."

"Just keep him from always saying Jesus," Talbot

mumbled. "And don't let him stand anywhere near Merlot. They have the same swagger."

"Richard is long gone. No one else in this town will balk at the fact you have a son. They won't make the connection." Weezer kept her gaze on Corbin.

"They will make a big deal about you doing the race with him." Carter appeared in the foyer and took the salad bowl. "We've been trying to talk her out of this idea all day. But she believes it's the best way to win." Carter leaned closer. "She's heard Silas is going to cheat and she figures this is the best way to beat him at his own game."

"Claudia is entered with Silas." Talbot swallowed. "This isn't a good idea."

"Richard is bogged down with so much bullshit right now, he might not even make a bid for the governor. We have him by the balls." Merlot strolled across the room. He gave Corbin a manly slap on the back before leaning in and gently kissing Talbot.

It was short and sweet, but it did the trick.

"Are you on board with this dumb idea?" she whispered.

"Absolutely not," Merlot said. "I'm just trying to look on the bright side. But you know my mom. Sometimes there's no reasoning with her and she's petrified she will lose to Mrs. Cummings."

"Who's that?" Corbin asked.

"A crazy woman," Weezer said. "Come on. Everyone is outside. Let's go introduce you to the family."

Corbin glanced over his shoulder. "Mom, help."

"You wanted a big family, kiddo; well, you got one," Talbot said.

"Maybe we should go save him." Merlot laced his fingers through hers and tugged her toward the family room.

"He'll be fine. He's actually been looking forward to this all day and I wanted a moment alone with you."

"Really?" Merlot smiled.

"To talk." She pursed her lips. "He still has a lot of questions, but mostly about us and why we can't be together."

"And what did you tell him?"

"The truth."

"Good." Merlot nodded.

"But it got me thinking." She plopped back on the sofa.

He sat down. "About?"

"We can't be together as a family in Candlewood Falls. That would be insanity. But we could almost anywhere else."

He palmed her cheek. "No, Talbot. We can't."

"Why not?"

"It would be too risky and we'd be constantly looking over our shoulders. But you're asking me to leave my family and never to see them again, because the only way that would work is if I do what you did."

She leaned her head against his. "I know. It's a dumb idea."

"It's not dumb, just crazy." He chuckled. "I have to admit, I thought about it too."

She jerked her head. "Don't mess with me, Merlot. I can't handle that."

"If there were a safe way for us to be together without either of us losing anything, I'd do it. I want to be with you. With Corbin. I care more about the two of you than I do anything else."

"But you care about your family too."

"I can't leave and you know that." He brushed his lips over her mouth, slipping his tongue inside, swirling it around in a wild dance. In this moment, he knew he'd never love another woman. She was it. The one. The only one. "Kisses sweeter than wine."

"Don't make me cry."

He cupped her chin. "My dad is hopeful about what the Department of Justice is doing regarding

Richard. Maybe for once in our lives, we'll get lucky."

Merlot

Merlot leaned against the tree trunk and watched his son toss a football back and forth with TJ as a couple of the toddlers and Riesling's daughter ran around his legs.

Corbin laughed as he tried to shake them off.

"That's a sight." His father handed him a beer.

Merlot swiped at his eyes before taking the cold one. "I became a father to a man who has an inch on me."

"He's almost as tall as me," his dad said with an exuberant pride. "Your mother might have told him one too many stories about you, so be prepared."

"After everything that has happened in these last few weeks, I think I can handle almost anything."

"Why don't I go grab all the little ones and you and Corbin can have some time alone before dinner." His father took two steps.

"Hey, Dad."

"What?"

"I know it's just a name, but Talbot didn't know about Grandma or your issues with her. I was in a mood the night I mentioned the name and she was trying to hold on to a piece of me."

His father smiled. "I like it. And honestly, it's kind of a fuck you to my mom and we both know she deserves it."

Merlot laughed.

Corbin tossed the ball to his grandfather and then crossed the yard where Merlot had positioned himself on a log.

"Having a good time?" Merlot asked.

"Interesting group of people," Corbin said.

"That is pretty much an understatement."

"TJ told me his entire life story. Man, I thought what I just learned about my life was messed up."

"That kid has been through the wringer, that's for sure. But my sister and Toby have done an amazing job helping him adjust."

"Dax said he's quite the hockey player." Corbin turned. "And holy shit. I grew up watching him play in the NHL. Now I understand why my mom got frustrated with my fascination for him."

"I'm sure anything remotely related to Candlewood Falls would wig her out."

"Can I ask you something?" Corbin sat cross-legged on the ground.

"Anything." Merlot joined his son.

"Why didn't you ever get married or have kids? I know why Mom never did. She was always busy with work and raising me. You had no idea I even existed. You had nothing tying you down."

"It took me years to get over what I thought was the death of your mother and the truth is, I never put it behind me."

"Why is that?"

"I'm not sure I have a logical answer."

"But you had to have dated. Had other relationships."

Merlot laughed. "Other than your mom, I have shit taste in women."

"My mom is kind of the best."

"You won't hear me argue with that," Merlot said. "I know this has been a lot for you to take in and my family has got to be overwhelming."

"Are you kidding me? When I was a little kid, I pretended strangers coming into the hotel were my long-lost family. This is great. I know I can't tell anyone. I'm used to that. I can't tell my mom half the shit I do in the military. Even if I could, I wouldn't. It would keep her up crying all night."

Merlot tapped his chest. "I might have only known about you for a short time, but that statement right there will send me worrying for the rest of my life."

"Wonderful." Corbin rolled his eyes. "My point is —and I hope you won't take this the wrong way—my mom was always enough for me. I might have always wanted to know who you were and why you didn't want me."

"Correction. If I had known about you, I would have fought like hell to keep you and your mom in my life."

"Fair enough." Corbin nodded. "I wanted to know you because that piece of the puzzle was missing for me, but not the same way as it was for my mom. The few times I saw her date, she was never really interested. She did it because Mama C and I pushed her into it. We thought her sense of sadness came from not having a partner. Not because she was missing all this." Corbin waved his hand toward the house before tapping his finger in the center of Merlot's chest. "And you. I thought some of her pain was because some man had broken her heart. Not some fucked-up situation that tore apart two people who obviously still love each other."

"You are a wise young man." The fact that Merlot

had missed Corbin's first twenty-one years no longer mattered. He'd find a way to stay in touch, no matter the future.

"I don't know about that. My previous master sergeant thought I was a wise ass with a chip on my shoulder."

"You have the River sense of humor and I can tell you there isn't a member of this family who doesn't carry that same chip."

"I can see that." Corbin shook his head. "And Weezer—my grandmother—kind of resents my name."

Merlot burst out laughing. "Yeah. That's one of life's cruel jokes. But don't take it personally. I should have told your mother the story behind the name."

"Weezer had no problem telling and now she calls me Corbie. That's annoying."

"It could be worse."

"I don't see how."

"My dad didn't want to name us kids after wines. It was a bone of contention with him for years. So, for a long time, he called me Merlie. Then it was Merlin. When I went to grade school, all the kids called me Merlin the Merlie. It took until middle school to break that one."

"Jesus. That sucks. How did you get everyone to call you Merlot?"

"Oh. I didn't. It took my mother to show up at career day with a shotgun."

"My God. I don't know what's worse."

"It gets better. My older brother and sister already struggled with having friends. Outside of the Wilde family and Dax, they didn't have any because the world was terrified of Weezer. So, when she did that, my few friends were no longer allowed to hang out with me, but they did call me by my first name. And they were equally afraid of me. Except for one kid."

"Who was that?"

"Your mother."

"That has got to be about the dumbest, saddest, sweetest story I've ever heard," Corbin said.

"Your mom and I were inseparable after that. But her dad hated my father. Which meant he despised me." Merlot ran a hand over his face. "If only your mom had told me sooner."

"Abuse is a terrible thing and I'm pretty sensitive to it." Corbin picked up a piece of grass and fiddled with it. "I had a close friend in high school who came out as transgender. It didn't change how I felt about her—well, him before she came out—but her dad thought he could beat it out of her."

"Jesus," Merlot muttered.

"My mom went ballistic. Her and Mama C called the cops. Shit. So much of my life makes sense now that I've met you and everyone here."

"I want you to know that no matter what happens, you've always got a place here. I know that we can't shout it from the rooftops right now, but I want to have some relationship with you."

Corbin nodded. "I'd like that too. I'd also like to help put this Richard guy behind bars."

"There isn't anything you can do."

"But there is," Corbin said. "My mom has always been humble about what I do. I think it's because it scares her."

"I haven't had much time to learn much about you or your career in the military. I know what you told me last night, but we spent most of it discussing my past."

"I graduated from high school when I was seventeen. A year early. I did one year of regular college and dropped out. My mom was pretty pissed about that. But regular learning wasn't for me, so I enlisted, but under the pretense I'd be fast-tracked for a career in Special Forces."

"She did not tell me that." Merlot jerked his head back. This was not a secret, but he would have liked to have known.

"At first, she didn't want me to do it. She has warmed up to the idea in the last year since I got my degree. My next stop is Ranger School. I hope to end up in Delta Force."

"That's mighty impressive." Merlot's chest swelled with pride.

"I feel like it's what I was born to do. Anyway, I got lucky and my last assignment was with a JSOC team. It was commanded by someone high up in the CIA. I don't see why I can't give him a call. He's a great man and had been a mentor to me these last few months."

"You're awfully young to be doing such things, aren't you?"

"I'm a bit of an overachiever."

"Well, that you don't get from me." Merlot laughed. "I'm lucky I graduated from college with halfway decent grades."

"Let me call Tom. We can trust him, I promise. You and your dad can be on the call with me. I want to help end it so my parents can have their happily ever after."

All the air in Merlot's lungs flew out like a bird

taking flight. "Let's go find your grandfather and see what he has to say about this."

"Perhaps we shouldn't tell Mom."

"Nope." Merlot shook his head. "I'm not keeping secrets from that woman. I watched too many lies almost destroy my parents and too many of them nearly broke me."

"You're kind of afraid of her, aren't you?"

"I saw a side of her yesterday when she spoke to you that absolutely terrified me, so yeah. Just a little."

Corbin laughed, jumping to his feet. "Fair enough. Oh, and one more thing."

Merlot stood, though not quite as swiftly as his son. "What's that?"

"Not that I'm ready to do this, because it would be even weirder than everything that's happened in the last day. Plus, I shouldn't get used to it because it would be dangerous. But when the day comes that all this is behind us, and it feels right, any problem with me calling you Dad?"

"Jesus. God, no."

"Damn. We sound alike."

"I know," Merlot said. "It's making my mom batshit because I'm the most like my dad and now she's got three of us to deal with."

"Something tells me I'll have fun with that."

"Oh, hell yeah." Merlot looped his arm around his son. Even though he couldn't share this with anyone other than his family, that didn't matter because family was all he cared about.

No matter how much Carter loved Weezer, there were moments he wanted to hog-tie her to the bed, and not for sexual reasons.

"Weezer's going down," Silas said as he approached Carter near the starting line of the three-legged race. "I don't care what young kid she brings in as a ringer, she's not winning this year."

"Why the hell do you care?"

"Because she cheats," Silas said.

"And you don't?" Carter laughed, then winked.

"All is fair in love and war." Silas smiled. "Claudia was surprised to see Talbot's son and I have to say, Weezer makes a big deal about family only. I'm shocked she's not using Dax or even Toby this year."

"The kid just landed Stateside. She's doing her

good deed for the year. She's got to get it out of her system so she can return to living up to her reputation."

Silas patted Carter on the back. "I wish I could come back with some nasty-ass retort, but we both know Weezer ain't bad. Except she cheats."

Carter shook his head. It was the same thing every damn year. "Ty Wilde and Riley Reynolds is an exciting lineup. You should worry more about them than Weezer and Talbot's son."

"I'm not worried about winning. I don't want Weezer to. It's the principle of the thing. See ya at poker."

"Bring a wad of cash, because I'm taking it."

"Yeah. Yeah." Silas meandered toward Claudia, who huddled next to Talbot and Corbin.

So far, other than the questions regarding the change in lineup, not a single person questioned or mentioned Corbin's family resemblance. However, all the males in the family kept their distance, including the grandkids. The only one who knew the truth was TJ, but he knew better than to expose this secret. He'd been through his own trauma thanks to his birth mother exposing Chablis' private medical records and what that had done to his family, not to mention his own life. That kid was as good as they came and Carter was proud to call him grandson.

Carter glanced over his shoulder and nearly fell.

He wiped off his sunglasses and blinked.

No fucking way. It couldn't be.

But there stood Richard, trying to hide himself. The only reason Carter knew it was him was because the fool had taken off his hat, showing off his bald fucking head. He pulled out his cell and texted Malbec. No point in unnecessarily worrying Merlot if by chance he was wrong.

But he doubted it.

Malbec texted back immediately, stating he'd scope out the situation and get back to him.

Carter lined up the racers. He hated doing this, but for some reason, the town thought he'd be some impartial judge.

Right.

Everyone cheated.

As soon as everyone took off, he checked his cell.

Fuck. His suspicions were correct. Fucking Richard. The man was crazy, but if he had come to Candlewood Falls, then Carter worried his biggest fear could be materializing and Talbot's identity was in jeopardy, if it hadn't already been compromised.

He texted Malbec back to keep an eye on Richard

while he dealt with this stupid, meaningless race that meant so much to Weezer for whatever reason.

He cringed as Ty plummeted into the water, but only after Weezer had tripped them.

Then Weezer and Corbin stumbled while Silas picked up Claudia, flew by, and crossed the finish line.

Carter jogged over to Weezer, helping her up. "Corbin, go find your mother. We're all going back to the vineyard for a celebration."

Weezer glared at him with a narrowed stare.

"Aren't there more games and shit?" Corbin asked.

"Weezer's a bad loser, so it's best if we go home, right, honey?"

"If you say so," she said, giving him the stink-eye.

"I think it's best." Carter winked.

"What the hell was that about? And fucking Silas cheated and you watched it happen," Weezer said.

"And I saw you trip Ty Wilde and said nothing, so it's all even." Carter wrapped his arm around her waist and kissed her temple.

"I can't believe we lost. We always host the Holiday Showcase."

"We have bigger problems than your ridiculous rivalry with Mrs. Cummings."

"Yeah, like what? Because that's a pretty big deal in my book."

"Promise me you won't look to your left, but Richard is standing in the crowd, incognito, and he's glaring at Talbot and Corbin."

Weezer paused midstep, but to her credit, she didn't shift her gaze. "You've got to be fucking kidding me? Why didn't we know he was in town? Doesn't he come with like a bodyguard, and he's always such a press whore."

"I have no idea why I didn't get a heads-up, but the fact he's hiding behind a baseball cap, ratty clothing, and sunglasses that make him look like a fucking idiot gives me a bad feeling."

"What are we going to do?"

"Malbec has been keeping an eye on him. I've called a buddy of mine at the local PD to see if he can put a tail on Richard. I've sent a text to the family group chat, telling everyone that we're having an impromptu gathering at the house. Just us. And that it's mandatory. That way, I can manage the situation and keep everyone safe, for the time being."

"I take it you included Talbot and—"

"They're family. Of course, I did. However, I didn't want to spook anyone, so I told them I had a big announcement."

"Oh shit. They will expect you to get down on one knee and propose."

"Would that be such a bad thing?" He chuckled.

"Yes. Because we're not doing that again. When we do get married, it will be without fanfare and I will not stand for some dumbass cheesy proposal like you did the last time."

"Okay. Then how about this? Just fucking marry me already."

"That works."

"It's about fucking time," he said.

Merlot

There had never been a time in Merlot's life when his father had ordered a family gathering that bad news hadn't been delivered. By the grim expression on his father's face, he expected this wouldn't be any different.

"What's going on?" Merlot took Talbot's hand and sat on the big sofa in the living room. Corbin sat on the other side of Talbot and his parents planted their asses on the fireplace.

Everyone else had been banished to the kitchen or outside under the pretense of taking care of the little ones or cooking food.

"There's no way of easing into this, so I might as well get down to business." His dad stretched out his legs and crossed them at the ankles. "Richard was at the Founders' Day picnic."

Talbot gasped. "No," she whispered. "Did he see me? My son?"

"I'm guessing he did," Merlot's father said. "I checked my email as soon as we got home, and I got a boatload of intel from Corbin's contact at the CIA. None of it good news."

"What did Tom get you?" Corbin asked.

"Mostly confirmation of everything we already knew. But Tom found out some disturbing information that we need to deal with." Merlot's father let out a long breath.

That was never a good sign.

"Andy doesn't own the house Talbot is renting. It's owned by a shell company," his father said.

"Who's behind that?" Merlot asked, only he already knew the answer.

"Her father," his mother said, confirming his suspicions.

"Jesus." Corbin inched closer to his mom on the sofa, wrapping his arm around her shoulders.

Merlot had wanted to do that, but he understood his son's need to comfort Talbot. He also appreciated the love the boy had for his mom.

"What we don't know is what or who could have tipped him off regarding the tenants," his mother said.

"I complained about how dirty the house was when I first got here. That's when Brad and Lyra came over. They helped me clean it up," Talbot said.

"The twins and I moved a lot of the old furniture out and moved in the stuff that Brad was getting rid of," Merlot added.

"Andy wasn't happy about that when he showed up a few days later, snapping pictures. He said he needed it for future rentals, but all he did was bitch about how I had no right. I told him I thought Brad and Lyra had his blessing." Talbot gripped Merlot's thigh.

"We all know Brad wouldn't just do something without at least trying to deal with Andy. He and Lyra had to put up with his shit when she was living there." His mother stood.

"Richard has been dealing with a lot of backlash. He knows he's about to be indicted on felony sexual assault charges. Assault. And campaign fraud. All of that is coming together. He's running scared. The problem is it brought him right back to Candlewood Falls and my front door," his father said. "Tom further discovered that Richard has been trying to poke around into my practice and my life. That makes this entire family fair game. He has no one in his pocket here, but that doesn't mean he hasn't been watching."

"Fuck," Merlot muttered. "Is it possible he never left town?"

"I'd say that's highly probable." His father nodded. "Zinny is on bed rest, so she and her family will stay here. Riesling, Trey, and their family can stay at Trey's biological father's house. No one would dare mess with them there. But that leaves everyone else we've got to figure out. I don't want anyone alone. I don't trust that man as far as I can spit."

"I can call in some reinforcements," Corbin said. "My entire team is on leave, plus I know some other guys. But it will take a day to get people here."

"If you can make that arrangement, I won't say no," his father said. "For now, we hang tight. If we have to all crash here for a night, we'll make it work."

"That's a lot of people under one roof," Merlot said. "I can make some calls to some old friends I know. I can at least get a few guns to stand guard."

"Do it," his father said. "On a brighter note, Mom and I are getting married."

"Not anytime soon." His mother glanced over her shoulder and glared.

"We're getting married. I proposed in a way that was agreeable to you and you accepted, so I'm holding you to that promise, woman." His father stood and planted a wet one on his stunned mother's lips.

"Your parents aren't married?" Corbin asked.

"No. They divorced before the twins and Zinny were born," Talbot said.

Corbin stuck his finger in his ear and wiggled it. "They are his though, right?"

Merlot laughed. "It's a very long and convoluted story, but yes. And my parents have always been a couple, but they couldn't live together for many years. Obviously, they never stopped having sex."

"I don't need to know about my grandparents' love life," Corbin said.

"Not to make this conversation any weirder, but I'm spending the night with your mother. I mean, it's for protection and all," Merlot said.

Corbin smacked his hand against his forehead. "On the one hand, that makes me ridiculously happy. On the other hand, your delivery is highly inappropriate when speaking to your child."

"You're a grown man. Serving in the Army. I think it's safe to assume you've had sex. Or do I need to have that conversation with you?" Merlot asked.

"Jesus. Please don't," Corbin said.

"Oh my God. The two of you are impossible." Talbot shook her head. "But at least the mood is lighter."

"Hey, Mom," Merlot called. "Does everyone else know about your pending nuptials?"

"No. And we're not going to tell them," his mother said.

"Oh, yes, we are." Merlot reached across the sofa and slapped Corbin's shoulder. "Go tell everyone the news."

"Corbie. Don't you dare," Merlot's mother said.

"Keep calling me that, and I'll do exactly what my father just asked me."

Merlot glanced to Talbot, his heart thumping in his throat.

Talbot wiped away a tear.

"Fine. I'll never call you that again." His mom folded her arms around her middle.

"I've got no skin in this game. I'll go tell them," Talbot said, jumping to her feet. "Sorry, Weezer. It's about time you and Carter officially tied the knot again." She scurried off toward the kitchen.

"I'm not giving you the recipe for my mac and cheese," Weezer scoffed.

"No worries. I've got it." Merlot smiled.

"Traitor." Weezer shook her head.

"I love this family," Corbin said with a serious expression. "I won't let that asshole come back into my mother's life and hurt her again. Or any of you."

"I'm afraid he'll come after you to get to your mom." Merlot's father strolled across the room. "I appreciate you calling in your friends. Having highly trained professionals in the area can't hurt. But I still don't want you out in that house alone, especially after what we just found out."

"No offense, Grandpa, but I graduated top of sniper school. No one is getting past me," Corbin said.

Merlot's father patted his chest. "Let me first get through the emotions of being called Grandpa, but yeah, no. I won't allow anyone in my family to be alone."

"We won't be. I've already heard from two buddies. They are both only two hours away. They will be here by nightfall. One can stand watch here. I'll put the other man wherever you want. But I can take care of my parents." Corbin puffed out his chest.

Merlot couldn't be any prouder.

"What on earth are we talking about?" Talbot came back into the room. She stood next to Merlot.

"Your son has a crazy idea," Merlot's father said.

"I beg to differ. I'm good at my job." Corbin narrowed his stare.

"I'm sure you're more than capable. But I won't be sleeping as it is and you're who I'm most worried about." His father placed a hand on Corbin's shoulder. "This is personal and that makes everything different."

"I respect that, but if he's coming after us, then let him. No better way to catch him at his own game, than to draw him out." Corbin arched a brow. "I'd rather force his hand than sit around and wait for him to make the first move."

"He's right, Dad," Merlot said. "Everyone in this family will be safer if Talbot, Corbin, and I are elsewhere. We all know I'm a good shot. So, why sit around and wait for Richard to come to us. Let's get this over with. Leak the information to Richard. Let him know Daisy's—"

"That's your real name?" Corbin interrupted Merlot. "I think I like Talbot better."

"So do I," Merlot said. "Anyway, give Richard the intel."

"I'm not putting your lives in danger," his father said sternly.

"I can't believe I'm going to say this, but I'm tired of living in fear that someday he will find me. My son has his father. His family. I don't want to lose this again. I won't let him run me out of the only place that has ever really mattered to me." Talbot squeezed Merlot's hand.

"I'll need forty-eight hours to put a plan into play before you let Richard in on our little secret," Corbin said. "Until then, we make sure we know where that bastard is."

"The only problem with that is we don't know if he has eyes on us," Merlot said.

"Let me do some recon around the places that everyone is staying. I'll set up some booby traps. We'll know if anything wonky is happening. Once I've got a team assembled, we'll set a trap and nail that bastard." Corbin pulled his mother close. "Trust me."

"I can live with this plan," Merlot said. "And it's my family who's most at risk. It's my call, Dad. Not yours."

His father nodded.

"Then it's settled," Merlot said. "And right after this is taken care of, we have a wedding to plan."

Talbot jerked her head.

"Not ours. My parents. But maybe someday in the near future we can discuss that."

"I haven't slept with you in years," she mumbled. "And the last time that happened, he happened." She poked Corbin in the arm.

"Jesus, Mom. Too much freaking information, but damn, what the hell are you two waiting for?" Corbin shook his head. "I'll sleep in my truck tonight to give you some privacy."

"That's my boy," Merlot said.

"Stop. Just freaking stop." Corbin stormed out of the room.

"Being a parent is kind of fun." Merlot wrapped his arm around Talbot. "But he's not sleeping in his truck."

"You might be sleeping on the sofa if you're not careful." She lowered her chin.

"Yes, ma'am."

12

TALBOT

Talbot pulled back the covers—to both sides of the bed. Her heart raced as she climbed on top of the mattress. She glanced down at her pathetic excuse for pajamas. Her tank top and shorts weren't ugly but couldn't be considered sexy.

What the hell was she thinking?

The door squeaked, and Merlot sauntered in with a smile. "Hey, you."

"I don't know if I can do this," she blurted out. "Our son is on the sofa down the hall watching a movie and eating popcorn."

"Actually, he just stepped outside with his rifle to go do rounds."

She groaned. "Not the point and not helping."

Merlot eased next to her, resting his hand on her

bare leg. "We don't have to do anything. I can take the guest room and have Corbin take the couch. Or the other way around."

"I'm afraid if we do that, we'll disappoint our son. When I said good night, he seemed so happy about you and me being a couple again."

"This shouldn't be about him. If we're going to be together, it should be because we want it."

She took his hand and pressed it against the center of her chest. "I do want you. That's not what I'm saying. This is just awkward. Not only did Corbin tell me he approved, but he gave me a lecture on safe sex."

Merlot burst out laughing.

"It's not funny."

"Oh, yes, it is." He leaned back, stuffing his hand in his pocket. "Especially when he handed me these right before he strapped his weapon over his shoulder." He held out three condoms. "I should be thrilled he thinks his old man has the stamina, but I had no idea what to say for a few seconds."

"He's always been a bit of a class clown. He's like Zinny that way." She took the foil packages and set them on the nightstand.

"I'd have to agree with that statement," Merlot

said. "I'm amazed at how quickly he's accepted everything."

"He's always been very adaptable. However, he will dig his heels in if he disagrees with something. He can be stubborn as hell."

"I have noticed that." Merlot's fingers danced across her skin. "I need to know something."

"Okay." She stared into his warm, loving eyes.

"Let's say we take care of Richard, would you consider staying in Candlewood Falls?"

She palmed his face. "Is that really a question you have to ask?"

He took her hand and kissed it. "Yes."

"I want to move back here. I have no idea what I'd do for work, so that's a problem, but if the stars align and my dad goes to prison, there isn't any place on earth I'd rather be."

"First, I already offered you a job, so that's taken care of." He ran his thumb over her lip. "And secondly, don't you think we should take a test drive and make sure we're still compatible?"

"Did you seriously just say that?"

"It came out a little sideways." He arched a brow. "It's a little strange we're talking about a future together after twenty-one years and we haven't even gone out on a date, much less shared a bed."

She waggled her finger. "My memory is a little fuzzy, but I did spend the night in your arms recently."

He shook his head. "I'm trying to be serious. I've never stopped loving you. If it's possible, I might love you more now than I did when we were teenagers. But there are things about us that are different and we can't expect to pick up where we left off."

"I don't think that's what we're doing." Feeling more confident in herself and her decision, she tugged at his shirt. "We're giving ourselves a fresh start. We're doing whatever it takes to ensure we have a chance at starting over. Isn't that why we're letting our son put himself in the line of fire?"

Merlot nodded as he tore off his T-shirt, tossing it across the room.

"For the record, we do need to use those." She pointed to the condoms. "I'm not on any birth control."

"Good to know and super glad our kid came prepared, although that sentence is a bit of a mood killer."

She laughed. "Can you not mention him again for a little while? Because if you keep doing that, you won't get lucky."

"I'm already lucky." He jumped to his knees, yanked her by the legs, and shoved her down on her back. "Do you remember the last time we did this?"

"Like it was yesterday." She shimmed out of her shirt, exposing her breasts.

He groaned. "I think they're bigger."

"I'm old and fat."

"Neither one of those things is true." He pressed his hot lips on her stomach. "I might have gotten a little better with age."

"Don't make me jealous of all the women you've been with, especially that bitch Rachel."

"Please don't ever bring her up again." He lifted his head. "And how do you think I feel?" He rolled her nipple between his thumb and forefinger.

Biting her lower lip, she arched her back. Every nerve ending in her body ignited under his touch. Her mind catapulted back to when she'd been a teenager and he'd explored her body for the first time. He'd been her first everything and she'd never forgotten.

He tugged at her shorts, pulling them and her panties to her ankles. "I'm so grateful to have you back and I don't plan on ever letting you go."

She never wanted to leave Merlot again but feared she'd have to.

"Hey." Merlot eased in next to her, pulling her tight. "Stop worrying about Richard. We're handling this and we will finally be able to be the family we were meant to be."

She threw her arms around Merlot, pushing every negative thought to the back of her brain. This was not the time or place. No matter what happened, this was about reconnecting with the only man she'd ever loved. She needed him. Wanted him.

He kissed her, hard and with the kind of passion that came out of love. There was no denying it had never died. She felt it to her core. Her body came alive in ways it hadn't in years.

"I have always loved you, Talbot," he whispered.

She loved that he used the name that had become her identity. He bridged the gap between the teenager she once was and the woman she'd become. To her, it meant that he'd accepted their current reality. A name was just a name.

He rolled her to her back, dotting tender kisses down her stomach while his hands toyed with her breasts.

Her breath caught in her throat.

"You are so beautiful." He pressed his mouth over her intimately.

Raising her hips, she gasped. The pleasure he brought to her body was as if she'd sailed home.

He glided his fingers inside, stroking gently, lapping at her like a tender brush of a feather. It was pure torture and she loved every second.

Sexually, this and providing oral sex to a man had been the one thing she couldn't ever do. It had been the reason a few relationships had ended.

Her tummy tightened and twitched as he settled deeper inside, his tongue moving faster, increasing pressure.

She held on to the sensations rolling over her body. Gliding her fingers through his thick, dark hair that had grayed slightly at the temples, she glanced down, watching him bring her close to the purest form of gratification.

Curling her toes, she held her breath. She wanted it to last as long as it could. He'd done this to her many times before they'd had sex and he knew exactly what her body demanded. He never failed to deliver. He'd always been tender and unselfish, wanting to please her first.

He never demanded she touch him or take care of him like she'd heard her friends say their boyfriends had. It had humbled her and she had felt like she'd been the luckiest girl in all the world.

That hadn't changed.

"Oh, God." She gasped. Her breath came in the form of a raspy pant. She clutched his head, rolling her hips with his movement. Hyperaware they weren't alone in the house, she did her best to keep her moans soft, but her climax hit her like a fucking tidal wave. "Merlot, oh, my… yes, yes…" She dropped her head back. Her body shook and quivered. She tried to fill her lungs with oxygen but failed.

He kissed the inside of her thigh and smoothed his hand over her stomach. Lifting his gaze, he smiled. "You're amazing."

"I think that's my line."

Pushing himself from the bed, he undid the button of his jeans and lowered his zipper.

"Allow me."

He dropped his hands to his sides.

"The first time I did this, I was so afraid I would hurt you."

He chuckled. "I remember." He smoothed back her hair.

"I haven't done this, or what you just did, since."

Taking her chin with his thumb and forefinger, he tilted her head. "You're joking, right?"

"No," she said softly.

"Why not?" His sweet gaze tore through her system.

She'd always been able to tell him anything. As teenagers, they talked about everything. No topic had been left off the table. And when it came to the really big topics, like sex, they had always been honest with each other. "I felt like I would have been betraying you somehow. I know that's weird, but it was the one thing that I could hold on to that was just ours."

"I don't know if I find that ridiculously sweet or kind of sad." He leaned over and kissed her lips. "You deserve to be happy. To have pleasure in your life. That includes all the relationships you had. Doesn't matter that I don't like that we've both been with other people, but it doesn't mean I wouldn't have wanted you to have all the joys in life."

Carefully, she rolled his pants over his hips, tugging them down his legs. Her eyes widened. "Let's see if I remember how to do this."

"It's not that hard."

"Oh, yes, it is." She curled her fingers around his length as he kicked his jeans to the side.

He groaned. "That's not what I meant."

Staring at him, she ran her hand gently up and down, studying his body. He wasn't the same teenager she'd been with all those years ago. He'd filled out and his shoulders were broader than she remembered. But this was the same man she'd fallen in love with and still loved with her entire soul.

Cupping him, she flicked her tongue over the tip, gliding it up and down, enjoying the way his fingers felt on her head as he pooled her hair. She'd done this to him many times, but never while he'd been standing up. She loved that their exploration was a combination of new and old clashing in a ball of flames. A sense of wild empowerment filled her veins as she took him into her mouth.

"Jesus, Talbot," he muttered. His leg muscles stiffened.

She pressed one hand on this taut stomach. It twitched. She took as much as she could, easing him in and out slowly while keeping her gaze locked with his with reckless abandon.

He tugged her off, shoved her back on the bed, and collapsed next to her, breathless. He cupped her, gently rubbing his finger over her hard nub as he took her nipple into his mouth.

She reached for him, but he batted her hand away.

"I want to touch you more," she managed through a raspy breath.

"You do that, and I'll be a seventeen-year-old old all over again and we won't get to use the condoms on the nightstand." He thrust two fingers inside her with force.

"Oh, God." She arched her back. "That's not fair."

He rolled his tongue over her nipple. It tingled, sending a shock wave across her skin right down to her toes. He moved to the other one, sucking on it, hard.

Stretching out her arm, she found one of the condom packages. "Here."

He laughed. "Someone is being impatient."

"More like someone has me primed and ready. Now put it on."

"Yes, ma'am." He ripped open the foil and rolled the protection over himself.

With a little more aggression than she'd planned, she shoved him to his back and straddled his hips. Adjusting their bodies, she leaned over, resting her hands on the mattress, her breasts not far from his face, and took him inside. It was as if she'd put on her favorite pair of jeans and they fit perfectly.

He gripped her thighs, taking her nipple once again into his mouth as he raised his hips, pumping into her, filling her with his own need. It was fast, hard, and wild. It was everything she needed and more.

"Oh, Merlot. Yes," she cried out, her climax tumbling out of her body.

He cupped the back of her neck and kissed her mouth, shoving his tongue between her lips.

She swallowed his groan as his orgasm exploded like a bomb going off inside her.

His motions slowed and she collapsed onto his chest with a heavy sigh and the biggest smile that she didn't think she'd be able to wipe off her face.

Ever.

"I really do love you, Talbot." He tickled his fingers up and down her back.

Popping her head up so she could look him in the eye and do this right, she said, "I love you right back, Merlin the Merlie."

He burst out laughing. "Only you could get away with calling me that."

She covered his mouth. "Shhh, be quiet."

"Me?" He shoved her hand away. "You were loud enough for both of us."

Her cheeks heated.

He kissed her forehead. "I can still hear the television. I'm sure it's fine."

"Nothing worse than hearing your parents have

sex," she mumbled. "Except walking in on Weezer and Carter. That had to be the most embarrassing thing that ever happened to me."

"Why did you have to bring that up?" Merlot groaned. "Seeing my mom with her skirt hiked up in the kitchen while my dad scrambled to zip up his pants had to have been the worst day of my life."

"I guess that's what we get for skipping school." She laughed. "Your parents are adorable. I love them."

"The feeling is mutual." Merlot sat up and glanced around. "Please tell me you have a trash can in this bedroom."

"Nope. Down the hall and in the bathroom."

"Shit. I didn't want to have to deal with the evidence that way." He pulled back the covers. "Fuck me."

"I already did that."

"Wasn't using the words in that context." Merlot sighed. "The condom broke."

"That's not good." She bolted upright. "Corbin either happened because of that—"

"Or the two times we went without." He raked a hand across the top of his head. "Well, I do want a fresh start and I did miss the baby thing the first time around."

"Bite your tongue, Merlot River. I'm too old for that shit."

"Chablis is forty. That's two years older than you."

"Not even the point." She fell back and covered her eyes. "Not to bring up all the shit we're trying not to think about, but if my father—"

"Hey." Merlot pressed his finger over her lips. "I'm half joking. I know we have a lot of things to work out and we're just getting to know each other again. Besides, there isn't anything we can do about it now but wait."

"I hope this is all over soon. I can't deal with this crap any longer. I'm running out of money."

"I'm going to take care you." He wrapped his arms around her body and pulled her close.

For twenty-one years she lived in fear.

Merlot made her feel safe again.

13

———

MERLOT

Merlot slipped from the bed as quietly as he could, not wanting to disturb Talbot. He knew her mind weighed heavily with her father in town and she'd tossed and turned most of the night. He found his jeans, a fresh shirt, snagged his weapon, and tiptoed out of the room. The smell of coffee smacked his nostrils and startled his brain awake.

He passed the guest bedroom. The door was ajar so he poked his head in.

No Corbin. He wasn't on the sofa either.

Merlot entered the kitchen and poured himself some bitter brew from the fresh pot that Corbin must have made, but he wasn't anywhere to be found.

The back door rattled.

He reached for his gun.

"Whoa. Relax." Corbin set his rifle down, leaning it against the counter. "It's just me."

"Don't do that again." Merlot arched a brow. "I might not be a sniper, but I do know how to use this thing."

"Dumb question, but why go from being a parole officer to working at the winery?" Corbin took a cup from the cabinet and handed it to Merlot. "Better yet, why did you become a parole officer in the first place."

"Long story short, I got pissed off at my parents and my two older siblings and flew the coop." Merlot handed Corbin his coffee and went about finding the pancake mix and all the fixings. "When I started on my path in criminal justice, my dad figured I would be a lawyer. That was laughable. I thought about being a cop. Between all the corruption that had gone down in the local sheriff's office with Richard and a buddy of mine that was wrongfully accused of something, I wanted to right a few wrongs, but ended up in the parole office."

"Not everyone there carries a gun."

"Nope." Merlot nodded. "But I had some difficult

cases early on and learned quickly that a weapon wasn't bad."

"Have you ever had to use it?"

"Unfortunately, yes. Twice on the job and once as a civilian."

"You shot someone?" Corbin asked.

Merlot nodded. "Wounded two of my clients who drew on me first."

"And what about the third time?"

"Not something I like to talk about." Merlot measured out the mix and dumped it in the bowl. He'd only been twenty-six years old when he'd pulled into the gas station on the way home from work. "I witnessed an armed robbery. More like I was smack-dab in the middle of it. This asshole had a young mother and her toddler in a death grip while he pressed his gun to the mom's head. The dick face had already shot and killed the store owner. I knew he wouldn't hesitate. When I got a clean shot, I took it."

"Jesus," Corbin muttered. "It's one thing in war, but I can't imagine doing that."

"It fucked with my head for long time. In therapy it had come out that I had been terrified of missing and hitting the woman more than being upset over my actions. I had tried to talk him down and wait for backup, but it had escalated so fast."

"I'm sure she was incredibly grateful."

Merlot tapped the egg on the side of the bowl. "I still talk with her and her family every once in a while. They are good people." He added the water and began blending with a whisk. "Happy birthday."

Corbin laughed. "Now my mom won't get on my case for having a beer now and then."

"We can start the day off with a mimosa or some Irish coffee if you'd like."

"Nope." Corbin pulled his cell out of his back pocket. "I've been up most the night keeping an eye on things. I'll probably take a nap while my buddy takes over."

"When all of this is over, we'll have to go out and celebrate properly."

"That would be fun." Corbin smiled. "So, did you and Mom have a fun night?"

Merlot blinked. "I'm not having that conversation with you."

"Well, by the smirk on your face, I'd say you did."

"Jesus, you're worse than my mother." Merlot turned and ducked his head into the fridge. "Sausage or bacon?"

"Both," Corbin said. "What makes Weezer worse?"

"Again, not up for discussion."

"Why? Did she catch you and Mom when you were teenagers?"

Merlot found the griddle and plugged it in. "No." This kid was going to be the death of him.

"Then what?"

"My God, you are more persistent than I've ever been. You're like a dog with a bone." Merlot set two pans on the stove, heating them up for the meat.

"Come on. Tell me. It can't be that bad."

"You've met the rest of this family. Nobody has a filter, except maybe Uncle Malbec and Aunt Eliza Jane."

Corbin slumped his shoulders and sighed.

There were times Corbin seemed so grown up, which he was, but other times, like now, he had a childlike quality.

"I missed out on knowing all of you for my entire life. I'm just trying to get to know you and everyone else better," Corbin said.

The kid had him there. "Fine." Merlot waggled the spatula across the island. "But you have to promise me you'll never tell your mother because if you do, I can guarantee I'll end up on the sofa for days to come."

"I wouldn't want that, so my lips are sealed." Corbin lifted his mug, blew, and sipped.

"There's this cottage on the winery near the river. It's where I currently live. Malbec used to stay there when he'd come home from college, but your mom and I would use it as our hangout when he wasn't there. I wasn't supposed to, but since my brother left me with a key, I figured if my parents never knew, who cared."

"I take it Grandma knew."

It fascinated Merlot how Corbin would swap back and forth between calling his grandparents by their first name and Grandma and Grandpa.

"You'll learn that woman knows everything." Merlot laughed. "Anyway, before your mom came over, I went out there and set everything up. I stole a bottle of wine from the cellar and got cheeses and crackers. I made it up real nice and romantic. We lied and told my folks we were meeting our friends for a movie in town. I parked the car on an access road by the alpaca farm and your mom and I hightailed it to the cottage. When we walked in, my mom had changed a few things."

"Like what?"

"The first thing was she took back the bottle of wine and replaced with a six-pack of soda."

"That's a buzzkill," Corbin said.

"No big deal, but on the center of the bed, where I had placed rose petals, she left a box of condoms and note reminding me to use them."

"Sounds like Grandma and I have a lot in common." Corbin laughed.

"My turn to make you squirm." Merlot flipped the bacon and tested the griddle before pouring some batter on it. "One of them broke and it's possible you were conceived that night."

"Dude. I never needed to know that."

"You asked." Merlot laughed.

"I guess I did, but I at least I know you tried to be responsible."

"That time. There were two times we didn't, so it's possible that four nights before that we made you."

"Jesus." Corbin covered his ears. "The fact you remember this shit is disturbing as hell."

"I remember every detail about your mother."

"Dad, please just stop."

Merlot dropped the pancake batter. It landed on the floor, covering his bare feet.

"Was that too weird?" Corbin blinked. "I mean, it

just came out. I didn't even think about it. But I've fantasized about this kind of thing my entire life. I used to wait in the hotel lobby and see businessmen waltz in and picture them scooping my mother up and telling her that they wished they'd never left her and how much they wanted me."

Tears burned Merlot's eyes. "I'm sorry I wasn't there for you when you were growing up." He walked around the island, dripping batter from his feet.

"You didn't know."

"There is nothing I can do about the last twenty-one years. I can't bring those back. However, I do want you. You're my son. And no matter what happened, I loved you the second I learned about you. That's never going to change."

Corbin pushed his chair back and rose, his eyes filled with his own tears. "This is honestly better than anything I could have ever imagined." He wrapped his arms around Merlot. "Just don't get used to cheesy man hugs. They aren't my thing."

"Well, they're mine." Merlot hugged his son tight and he had no desire to let go.

"Mom's going to kill you. She's a shitty cook, but she hates a messy kitchen."

Merlot chuckled. Leave it to his kid to know

when a little humor could do the soul some good. He found the paper towels and dealt with his feet. "Here. You clean up the floor. I'll make more batter." He took the sausage and bacon out of the pans, and flipped the pancakes that were already on the griddle, grateful they weren't burned.

A phone dinged.

"That's Grandpa. Again." Corbin tossed the towels in the trash before lifting his phone. "He's been texting since three this morning."

"About what?" Merlot quickly mixed another batch.

"First to thank me for my buddy showing up. Then to check on when the rest of my friends were coming." Corbin sat down and lifted his gaze. "The last of them roll in around ten this morning. Grandpa said once he knows my men are in place, he'll have his guy in DC send the intel about Mom to Richard, and then it's game on. We both figure that should be around three, since he said Richard is an impatient fuck."

Merlot shoved a plate in front of his son. "Why are you just telling me this now? You should have either woken me up with this news, or at the very least started the conversation with it."

"Am I about to get my very first *Dad* lecture?"

Corbin cut into his pancake and dunked it in his coffee.

That was another thing Merlot did and everyone thought it was odd.

It was not so strange when he saw someone else do it, but it was weird that his son had picked up so many traits from him and he hadn't raised Corbin.

"I really want to say *don't get fresh with me,* but I think we're way past that." Merlot took his plate and eased onto the seat next to Corbin. "Just don't do that again. Our family is at stake and I won't lose you again."

Corbin's phone dinged once more. "My buddy said there's a dark sedan rolling into the driveway."

"That could be half a dozen people." Merlot snagged his weapon and holstered it in his jeans. "Stay put."

"I'll check the back." Corbin grabbed his rifle. "We have a blind spot there until the rest of my friends get here. That's why I stayed up all night doing recon every fifteen to thirty minutes."

Merlot peeked out the front window. Fucking Andy. That could only mean bad news. He pulled open the door and stepped outside. "Hey, Andy. What brings you by?"

"I'm here to see my tenant. Her rental agreement

is up tomorrow and I've got a lead on someone else to stay here."

Bullshit. Talbot had signed another two-week rental three days ago. Merlot knew this because he'd paid the bill.

"She's not here right now."

"Well, she needs to vacate the premises."

"That's crazy, Andy. She sent you money to extend her rental. You can't kick her out. Don't make me bring my father into this because you know I will."

Andy held up his hands. "Go right ahead. I'm well within my rights. Just give Ms. Grant my message." He hopped into his vehicle and backed out.

Fucking jerk. He wasn't there to send Talbot packing. He was there to let them know Richard was onto them.

Merlot stepped into the family room and froze, staring at Richard holding a gun to Talbot's head.

Talbot

Talbot felt a warm breeze coat her face. She stretched her arms. "Merlot?"

"You haven't changed. You're still a trashy little whore."

She pulled the covers to her chin and sat up straight. She blinked. No. She couldn't be staring at her father. How did he get in? Where was Merlot? Where was her son?

This couldn't be happening.

Play dumb. That's what Carter had told her to do if she bumped into him.

"Who are you?"

Her dad laughed. "That's fucking rich." He rummaged through her drawers and tossed some clothes at the bed. "Get dressed. We have four minutes to make it into the family room so I can surprise that pansy-ass boyfriend and son of yours."

"What have you done?" She clenched her teeth while she tugged the shirt over her head. "If you touch either one of them, it will be the last thing you do."

"You should have thought about that before you came back from the dead." He grabbed her by the arm and yanked her off the bed. "I couldn't believe it when Andy told me about this girl Talbot Grant who was renting a house that one of my companies owned who looked incredibly like my daughter. The picture he texted me sent me to my knees." He shoved her into the hallway. "I always knew you and your mother didn't die in that fire. I spent years trying to prove it, but fucking Carter thought he was smarter than me. Well, I'll have my revenge."

"Whatever you have planned, you won't get away with it."

"Yes, I will." He grabbed her around the waist and pressed the gun against her temple.

She gasped.

"Get your fucking hands off her." Merlot raised his weapon.

"I'd put that thing down," her dad said. "And before you go bragging about what a good shot you are, I do remember that man you shot, saving that young woman. But this isn't that situation. First, I'm trigger-happy, so shoot. I'll pull the trigger before the bullet hits me. Second, Andy isn't far away and he's not alone. That was just a decoy and he won't hesitate to shoot you in the back."

Merlot grimaced. His eye twitched. He lowered his aim. "I'm going to enjoy wrapping my fingers around your neck and watching the life suck right out of you."

"Kick that thing over here," her father said.

She took in slow deep breaths. Corbin had friends close by. She had to trust that Merlot had caved to her father's demands because he knew things she didn't.

Merlot set the gun on the floor and used his bare foot to send it flying.

"Now, where's that grandson of mine?" her father asked.

"You're no grandfather to me," Corbin's voice rang out.

Her father spun her around, squeezing her arm with all his might, the cold metal of the gun still hard against her temple.

"Well, looks like someone brought a bigger weapon, but that won't help you." Her father laughed. "Put it down, boy. In less than five minutes this place will be crawling with my people."

"Don't let my youth fool you." Corbin kept his gun pointed at her father's head. "I could squeeze the trigger and you wouldn't know what hit you."

"Maybe, but would you risk that with your precious mother so close?" Her father inched behind her, using her as a shield.

Her heart pounded in her chest. She'd always been afraid of her father and what he could do to her and her mom.

But now he threatened her son and the man she loved.

The madness had to end.

Merlot

Merlot heard boards creaking behind him. He glanced over his shoulder and saw a shadow slink across the front porch window.

If that had been one of Richard's men, they wouldn't be hiding. They would have waltzed right through the front door.

Merlot didn't know if Corbin had seen and heard enough about what had been going on to send a message to his grandfather and his friends. The original plan had been to set Richard up in a situation where they could record him discussing all the terrible things he'd done.

But that had included Merlot's father. Merlot didn't know half the things his father did. However, maybe he could get Richard talking.

With Richard's back to Merlot, he inched closer, shifting his gaze from Corbin to the gun on the floor.

Corbin slowly blinked. "There are at least four points of your body exposed. Trust me, I'd miss my mom by a mile."

Merlot leaned over, picked up his weapon, and tucked it behind his back.

"You're a cocky little shit," Richard said. "But I shouldn't be surprised since you are Merlot's son." He laughed. "It's so fucking obvious. You look just like him."

Corbin smiled. "I'm proud to call that man Dad."

"That's pathetic." Richard continued to cower behind Talbot. "Merlot, get your ass over here next to this ridiculous excuse for a human so I can see you."

Keeping his back to the wall, he sidestepped toward his son. "Tell me something, Richard. What's your plan? Because I can't imagine we're walking out of here alive."

"Yeah. I'd kind of like to hear that too." Corbin eased his gun to his waist.

"It's pretty simple. Lyra had lots of problems with the gas stove and Andy has a record of my daughter here complaining about this, that, and the other thing. He came by here today to check on things, but it was too late. The entire place was engulfed in flames from an explosion in the kitchen, thanks to a gas leak." Richard shook his head. "Such a shame that Merlot had to go the same way his beloved Daisy did. I wonder if they will do DNA and discover the truth about these two."

"This is so highly entertaining. I honestly can't believe you think you can pull this off. You don't look that bright," Corbin said.

"You're a smart-ass," Richard said.

"I take after my grandmother, Weezer." Corbin cocked his head.

Richard shoved the gun harder against Talbot's head.

"Motherfucker," Corbin mumbled. "I'm done with you, so unless you want to either be mortally wounded, or even better, six feet under, let go of my mother."

Merlot reached out, resting his hand on Corbin's shoulder. "Take it easy. I think we're about to be outnumbered. A car just pulled into the driveway."

"It's about time." Richard stretched out his arm. "Give me that fucking thing. I'm sick of looking at it pointed at my face."

Merlot squeezed Corbin's biceps.

Corbin released his finger from the trigger and hit the safety.

Smart fucking man.

"Sit down." Richard gave Talbot a violent shove toward the sofa.

She groaned, stumbling and tripping over the coffee table.

It killed Merlot that he couldn't race to her in that moment. He glanced to his son, who nodded.

Both Merlot and Corbin inched across the room.

Richard set the rifle on the floor and curled his fingers around the doorknob, yanking it open. "What the—"

Corbin jumped on Richard's back, tackling him to the ground.

Bang!

Talbot screamed.

Merlot's heart dropped as he yanked his weapon from his back. He watched in horror as Corbin tried to disarm Richard. Merlot found the right moment to kick Richard in the side.

He repeated the motion until he had the right angle to step on Richard's arm. "Drop it, asshole."

Corbin jumped to his feet. He yanked the weapon from Richard's hand and threw it across the room before taking him by the shirt. He cocked his fist and nailed Richard in the nose. He brought his hand back, winding up for a second punch.

"That's enough, Corbin," Merlot said. "Besides, you're bleeding."

Three men, all in Army fatigues, came racing into the room. Sirens blared out in the background.

Talbot was on her feet, patting Corbin down.

"Mom. I'm fine. That's Richard's blood. He's the one who got shot. Not me," Corbin said.

"Oh, thank God." Talbot threw her arms around her son.

"Get me a goddamned ambulance and you will all pay for this. Do you know what happens to people who shoot senators?" Richard curled up, gripping his gut. "I'm going to make sure you all rot in hell for this."

Merlot let out a big sigh of relief. He wrapped his arm around Talbot and stood over Richard, glaring down at the reason he'd been ripped from his family. The sole person who stole twenty-one years of his son's life. "I've got news for you. You're the one who will be decaying in a federal prison."

"That's never going to happen." Richard groaned.

"Think again, because the CIA has a file on you three inches thick. All you did by breaking into our home was give yourself an early demise because you were less than a week away from being arrested." Merlot tugged his son closer. "You can't hurt anyone ever again. And if you ever come near me or my family, I'll let my son put a bullet between your eyes."

"Don't encourage him." Talbot leaned into his body. "I need fresh air."

"Let's get out of here," Corbin said. "My buddies can watch this asshole while we wait for the authorities."

"They're already here." Merlot headed outside, ignoring the shouts coming from Richard.

It was over.

"Is there any way he could get away with this?" Talbot stared at him with fear in her eyes.

"Even if this doesn't stick, we've got so much more." Merlot kissed her temple.

"And I've got a secret weapon." Corbin smiled, pulling out his phone. "I recorded the entire thing and New Jersey is a one-party consent."

"How the hell do you know that?" Merlot asked.

"Grandpa told me. It was his idea." Merlot pulled him in for a man hug.

"Humph. Dude. I told you I'm not that guy." Corbin patted his back.

"Get used to it, and your grandfather's the same way. How about we find a better way to celebrate this young man's birthday?" Merlot looped his arm around the woman he'd love and the son he'd protect forever.

"Now, I'll take that Irish coffee," Corbin said.

"I need a shower and a change of clothes, but I have no desire to return to that house today." Talbot rested her head on Merlot's shoulder. "But I guess I'm moving to Candlewood Falls. That job still up for grabs?"

"You start on Monday." And for the first time in twenty-one years, everything in Merlot's life had aligned. "And I get to have kisses sweeter than wine every day."

14

CARTER
THREE WEEKS LATER...

"Over my dead body will I let you back out, woman." Carter planted his hands on his hips and stared at Weezer. She was the most infuriating and lovable human in his life. He couldn't imagine his world without her in it.

"Why does it matter if we get married? Our lifestyle has been working for us for years. I don't understand why you're forcing me to change it."

Carter shook his head and laughed. He shouldn't, because it might make this situation worse. "You made a promise to me." He held up his fingers. "Once when I moved back in and then again at the three-legged race, we'd do this. The only people who are here are our kids and grandkids."

"Carter, it's just a piece of paper. Hell, we had the

twins and Zinny without being married. We didn't even live in the same house."

"This is different." He cupped her face. "There were a million secrets that were tearing us apart. The only way our relationship would survive was if we separated." He took her by the hand. "Corbin ships out tomorrow and won't return for four months."

"We can do it then."

"His parents will most likely get married when he comes home the next time. I'm not going to take the spotlight away from them." He tugged her from their bedroom. "By the way, you look beautiful."

"I know."

"And there's the love of my life." He held out his elbow and guided her down the staircases and through the home where they'd raised their children. It had been in her family for generations. He thought it might be time to pass it down to Zinny and her family. She really wanted it and it was about time Weezer retired from the wine business altogether.

But he'd save that conversation for after they got back from a second honeymoon.

He opened the door for his bride and smiled.

Ashling, their granddaughter, came running over. "Grandma, Grandpa, you both look so amazing."

"Thank you, baby." Weezer leaned over and kissed the young girl.

"Here. Mommy said to give you this." Ashling pushed a bouquet of flowers at Weezer.

"My, my. Aren't these beautiful." Weezer sucked in a deep breath. "Okay, old man. Let's get this over with."

"It will be the fastest wedding you have ever attended."

"Better be, or you won't make it to the honeymoon."

Carter chuckled. "You've always made me the happiest man alive, even when you're being a pain in the ass."

Merlot

"Only my mother would have hot dogs and hamburgers at a wedding reception." Merlot tossed his paper plate in the trash in the kitchen.

"Grandma is unique." Corbin cut into the wedding cake, slapping a large piece onto a plate. "Those wedding vows were highly entertaining."

Merlot hadn't seen anyone, except maybe TJ, eat that much food in one sitting. "I'm just glad they did it. Next on the list will be to get her to retire and let Zinny and Toby move into this house."

Corbin's left eye twitched. He held his fork halfway between his face and the plate. "I've never lived anywhere but a hotel and now an Army base."

"I hope you will consider this home." Merlot rested his hand on Corbin's shoulder. "And not just because your mom is moving back here, but because you have family here that loves you and wants you to be a part of their lives."

"I would like that very much."

"So would I." Merlot smiled. "Now, have you seen your mother? She disappeared and has been acting strange all day."

"I noticed that too. She came in to use the bathroom like ten minutes ago." Corbin leaned against the counter, stuffing his mouth with cake. "Maybe it has to do with the property Mom was renting. Did you find anything out?"

Merlot nodded. "Grandpa is working on the legal shit now, but once all that is taken care of, I should be able to close on the property in thirty days."

"How is that possible?"

"The shell company that owns it is selling off

most of its assets. Richard has no backing anymore. He's bankrupt, literally. He can't even post bail. He's been blackballed everywhere and my parents are helping move some cash around so no one else tries to buy it out from under me."

"I read there are now fifteen women who are accusing him of sexual assault and they found a money trail from campaign donations to personal accounts he tried to hide in foreign countries."

"Yeah, he's fucked," Merlot said. "I'm sorry if all the hype is affecting your military career. As much as I'm proud for the world to know I'm your dad, I didn't mean for it to make national news."

Corbin set his plate on the counter and shrugged. "I guess the only bummer is my last name is Grant, not River."

Merlot cocked his head. "You know, you can change that. You'd have my blessing. And everyone in this family. But I'd talk to your mom before you do anything." He'd asked Talbot to forget about everything and marry him. They'd lost too much time, but she wanted to wait. She said she needed the time to ease back into Candlewood Falls and the reality check of people knowing her true identity. He wished he completely understood, but he didn't. They loved each other and through all the lies, betrayals, and years apart, it was as strong as ever. Their family and Claudia accepted them and Corbin as a unit. Making it official was all that Merlot wanted.

However, he'd have to be patient.

"I already did. She said I needed to float it by you."

Merlot opened his arms.

Corbin shook his head and hands. "Nope. We're not doing another man hug."

"Oh, yes, we are." Merlot slapped his son on the shoulders as he pulled him in tight. "You'll get used to this."

Corbin groaned. "I love you, Dad. But this, never."

Talbot slammed the bathroom door. Her lips were drawn into a tight line. She threw her purse on the counter. It knocked three plates on the floor.

"What's the matter?" Merlot asked.

"I blame your son." Talbot pointed to their son. "It's all his fault."

"Me? What did I do?" Corbin tapped his chest.

"You know what. You're both equally responsible." Talbot glared.

"Whatever it is, we should leave." Merlot snagged his beer from the kitchen table. For the last twenty-four hours, Talbot had been acting strange. He figured it was because Corbin was leaving in the morning. He wasn't being deployed, but he would be going to some major intensive training, which meant the next part of his journey in Special Forces would begin.

He understood how much that frightened Talbot. It scared him too, but this was important to his son and Merlot would support it.

"You're not going anywhere. We need to talk," she said.

"Okay. Sounds like my cue to see what's going on outside." Corbin lifted his beer.

"Nope. This affects you too." Talbot pulled out a stool and plopped herself on it. "And I don't feel like saying it twice and it should come from me. The rest of the family, your father can tell."

"What's going on, sweetheart?" Merlot massaged the back of her neck. He had no idea what ruffled her feathers. Whatever had gotten under her skin, he'd do whatever was necessary to make it right.

"I can't believe this is happening. It's freaking bizarre and you both oddly played a role in it." She tossed her hands in the air and they landed on her lap with a thud.

"What are we responsible for, exactly?" Merlot cringed, waiting for the answer.

"I'm pregnant." She sighed.

"Um, only he can be to blame for that." Corbin slapped Merlot on the back.

"Not true. The condom you gave me broke, kind of like how you were conceived all those years ago." Merlot pulled up a stool.

"I thought I liked how open this family was, but that is way too much information." Corbin laughed.

Merlot kept his attention on Talbot. "Are you sure?"

She dug into her purse and waved a stick under his nose.

He took it from her hands.

Corbin leaned over his shoulder. "Congrats. Looks like I get to be a big brother after all."

"I'm too old for this," Talbot whispered.

Merlot dropped his arm around her shoulders. He wanted this baby and not because he'd missed it all with Corbin. He loved his son and if he was the only child he had, then he'd be happy.

But to add new life to a fresh start was icing on the cake.

"No, you're not. And when Corbin comes home

in few months, we can have a small private wedding."

She cocked her head and glared.

He raised his hands. "If that's what you want. No pressure."

"It's not that I don't want to marry you. I do. In time. And I've been thinking about doing it when Corbin came home next. But now I'll be all fat and ugly by then."

"You'll be beautiful," Merlot said.

"Relax, Mom. It could be worse. I could have used that condom and you could be a grandma." Corbin smiled wide.

"Even I don't find that funny." Merlot arched a brow. "You better start checking the expiration date on those things."

"And let your dad buy his own because this"—she waved a hand over her stomach—"will be the absolute last time."

"Are you sure about that?" Merlot cocked his head. "My mom said that after me—"

"You hush your mouth, Merlot River. Or you won't ever get—"

"Not in front of the child." Corbin took his beer and strolled out the back door.

Merlot palmed her cheek. A trickle of fear swirled in his gut. "Are you happy about this?"

Her lips parted and tears filled her eyes. "Oh yes. I'm in shock, but I want this very much. I would have liked more time getting settled in my new job and in this family. And especially with us. But I love you, Merlot. It's always been you."

"Kisses sweeter than wine."

Thank you for reading KISSES SWEETER THAN WINE. Please feel free to leave an honest review.

If you'd like to know more about Claudia and Silas, please check out STEALING HEARTS by Stacey Wilk.

And to learn more about Riley Reynolds please pick up WILDE & DANGEROUS by K.M. Fawcett.

Jen Talty is the *USA Today* Bestselling Author of Contemporary Romance, Romantic Suspense, and Paranormal Romance. In the fall of 2020, her short story was selected and featured in a 1001 Dark Nights Anthology.

Regardless of the genre, her goal is to take you on a ride that will leave you floating under the sun with warmth in your heart. She writes stories about broken heroes and heroines who aren't necessarily looking for romance, but in the end, they find the kind of love books are written about :).

She first started writing while carting her kids to one hockey rink after the other, averaging 170 games per year between 3 kids in 2 countries and 5 states. Her first book, IN TWO WEEKS was originally published in 2007. In 2010 she helped form a publishing company (Cool Gus Publishing) with *NY Times* Bestselling Author Bob Mayer where she ran the technical side of the business through 2016.

Jen is currently enjoying the next phase of her life… the empty nester! She and her husband reside in Jupiter, Florida.

Grab a glass of vino, kick back, relax, and let the romance roll in…

Sign up for my Newsletter (https://dl.bookfunnel.com/ 82gm8b9k4y) where I often give away free books before publication.

Join my private Facebook group (https://www.facebook. com/groups/191706547909047/) where I post exclusive excerpts and discuss all things murder and love!

And on Bookbub: bookbub.com/authors/jen-talty

facebook.com/AuthorJenTalty

instagram.com/jen_talty

bookbub.com/authors/jen-talty

amazon.com/author/jentalty

pinterest.com/jentalty

Defending Raven

Fay's Six

Yellowstone Brotherhood Protectors

Guarding Payton

Candlewood Falls

RIVERS EDGE

THE BURIED SECRET

ITS IN HIS KISS

LIPS OF AN ANGEL

It's all in the Whiskey

JOHNNIE WALKER

GEORGIA MOON

JACK DANIELS

JIM BEAM

WHISKEY SOUR

WHISKEY COBBLER

WHISKEY SMASH

IRISH WHISKEY

The Monroes

COLOR ME YOURS

COLOR ME SMART

COLOR ME FREE

COLOR ME LUCKY

COLOR ME ICE

COLOR ME HOME

Search and Rescue

PROTECTING AINSLEY

PROTECTING CLOVER

PROTECTING OLYMPIA

PROTECTING FREEDOM

PROTECTING PRINCESS

PROTECTING MARLOWE

DELTA FORCE-NEXT GENERATION

SHIELDING JOLENE

SHIELDING AALYIAH

SHIELDING LAINE

SHIELDING TALULLAH

SHIELDING MARIBEL

The Men of Thief Lake

REKINDLED

DESTINY'S DREAM

Federal Investigators

JANE DOE'S RETURN

THE BUTTERFLY MURDERS

THE AEGIS NETWORK

The Sarich Brother

THE LIGHTHOUSE

HER LAST HOPE

THE LAST FLIGHT

THE RETURN HOME

THE MATRIARCH

More Aegis Network

MAX & MILIAN

A CHRISTMAS MIRACLE

SPINNING WHEELS

HOLIDAY'S VACATION

Special Forces Operation Alpha

BURNING DESIRE

BURNING KISS

BURNING SKIES

BURNING LIES

BURNING HEART

BURNING BED

REMEMBER ME ALWAYS

The Brotherhood Protectors

Out of the Wild

ROUGH JUSTICE

ROUGH AROUND THE EDGES

ROUGH RIDE

ROUGH EDGE

ROUGH BEAUTY

The Brotherhood Protectors

The Saving Series

SAVING LOVE

SAVING MAGNOLIA

SAVING LEATHER

Hot Hunks

Cove's Blind Date Blows Up

My Everyday Hero – Ledger

Tempting Tavor

Malachi's Mystic Assignment

Needing Neor

Holiday Romances

A CHRISTMAS GETAWAY

ALASKAN CHRISTMAS

WHISPERS

CHRISTMAS IN THE SAND

Heroes & Heroines on the Field

TAKING A RISK

TEE TIME

A New Dawn

THE BLIND DATE

SPRING FLING

SUMMERS GONE

WINTER WEDDING

THE AWAKENING

The Collective Order

THE LOST SISTER

THE LOST SOLDIER

THE LOST SOUL

THE LOST CONNECTION

THE NEW ORDER